"Amanda?" Stewart came up behind her, and his strong arms pulled her gently back against his chest so that she was close against him, still facing the crib.

His voice was low and determined. "The pneumonia was confirmed by chest X-ray. If it is bacterial then there is hope we should be able to beat it." His voice rumbled comfort in her ear. "The onset is very sudden, but we've started treatment now."

Both faced Simone as his hands eased down Amanda's shoulders to her upper arms, and he tried to infuse some of his strength into her. "Simone is very ill, but we're onto it. You and I will be here until she turns the corner. She's a fighter—like her mother."

Stewart was right. Simone was a fighter, and she, Amanda, would have to draw on that faith to keep strong. "I love you, Simone. Mommy's here." Her voice broke and she swallowed the fear and pain in her throat. She had to be strong for her daughter. "Hang in there, darling."

Stewart was always there in the background, quietly circulating the unit, unobtrusive, aware of every nuance of Simone's condition, keeping an eye on all the babies. Watching Simone. Watching Amanda.

Dear Reader,

I'm thrilled to present *Their Special-Care Baby.*

I hope you enjoy Stewart and Amanda's story. This is a special one for me because my granddaughter weighed just over a pound when she was born. The doctors and nurses who care for premature infants are miracle-makers in their own right.

Our own Simone is a bouncing two-year-old now, and to all those parents and grandparents who have lived through a similar premature-baby journey—I salute you.

Warmest regards,

Fiona McArthur

THEIR SPECIAL-CARE BABY
Fiona McArthur

HARLEQUIN®

TORONTO • NEW YORK • LONDON
AMSTERDAM • PARIS • SYDNEY • HAMBURG
STOCKHOLM • ATHENS • TOKYO • MILAN • MADRID
PRAGUE • WARSAW • BUDAPEST • AUCKLAND

ISBN-13: 978-0-373-19903-7
ISBN-10:   0-373-19903-1

THEIR SPECIAL-CARE BABY

First North American Publication 2008

www.eHarlequin.com

Printed in U.S.A.

TOP-NOTCH DOCS

He's not just the boss, he's the best there is!

These heroes aren't just doctors, they're life-savers.

These heroes aren't just surgeons,
they're skilled masters. Their talent and reputations
are admired by all.

These heroes are devoted to their patients.
They'll hold the littlest babies in their arms
and melt the hearts of all who see.

These heroes aren't just medical professionals.
They're the men of your dreams.

This book is dedicated in memory to my mother,
Catherine, whose beautiful smile and
"Hello Darling" will always warm my heart.

CHAPTER ONE

STEWART KRAMER leant on the over-track bridge
and waited for the Brisbane train to come into view.
He contemplated the fierce Australian sun as it
shimmered off the entwined silver rails on the track
and tried not to think about other things he should
have been doing instead of cleaning up after his late
brother.

As a child he'd imagined he might work on the
railway, anywhere away from Sean. Stewart was dis-
tracted by a commuter train that pulled in and then
headed back into Sydney.

A swarm of passengers flowed around him as they
crossed the coathanger-shaped pedestrian bridge then
surged down the stairs to road level.

Desiree's train had been delayed, luckily, because
a tiny set of twins had put his own arrival back an hour
while his team had worked to stabilise them in the
unit. He had a gut feeling about the larger twin that
he'd follow up if his registrar hadn't already, but his

thoughts were interrupted by the loudspeaker warning of the Brisbane train's impending arrival.

Desiree's latest mobile text message had suggested his newly acquired sister-in-law and baby niece were travelling in the second carriage from the driver's and he began to think of moving down to help her with the pram. No doubt she would be as helpless and fashion-brained as all his brother's women had seemed in the past.

No matter. He would look after them, and the new baby on the way. Even in death his older brother had left wreckage for Stewart to clean up.

He still couldn't believe that Sean was dead, despite the fact that his brother had danced with danger for so many years on the darker side of life and had then suddenly left a widow and children. Sean could have been so much more.

He wondered briefly if Desiree was her real name or the stage name she'd chosen before she'd married Sean.

The blue inter-city express suddenly appeared around the bend and Stewart straightened. The train seemed to be making up for its tardiness with an extra burst of speed as it passed the departing commuter train. The flyer resembled a blue ribbon in the wind as it streamed towards him and Stewart pushed himself off the rail and forced some enthusiasm for his new family.

Stewart glanced again at Desiree's train, and at

the edge of his vision a silver freighter continued to ease smoothly onto the track in front of the oncoming express as if it had all the time in the world.

Seconds slowed and the initial scream of brakes from the express did nothing but pierce the air with fruitless warning before the trains collided.

The explosion of two great forces meeting with a scream of metal on metal shrieked into the morning routine like an invasion from hell. Smoke and debris shot skywards confirming the sight his brain had dismissed as impossible.

Instinctively Stewart closed his eyes as the horrific scene grew to a pile-up of carriages he'd only imagined seeing as a child on his father's miniature line. This was no young boy's accidental manoeuvrings—this was adult folly of criminal proportions.

Stewart's mind recoiled at the thought of the damage such twisted metal would make on frail human flesh as he turned and scanned the bridge to gauge the fastest way to the tracks.

Adrenalin surged as his heart pounded in his chest and he took the stairs three at a time down to the platform. Somewhere in the wreckage his sister-in-law and niece would be lying, along with many others.

Stunned commuters stared without comprehension up the track at the jumble of carriages. A black pall of smoke hung in the morning sunlight and slowly, piercingly, a lone woman facing the catastrophe began to scream as Stewart vaulted down onto the track and began to sprint up towards the wreckage.

More bystanders must have joined him from the platform because he could hear the echo of running feet on the track behind him or maybe it was his own heartbeat pounding in his ears. Then everything seemed to slow as he came abreast of the devastation.

The engine on the freighter lay buried beneath the smashed driver's cab of the express and there was no way of sighting either driver. Stewart barely paused as he hurdled over debris and made his way to the first of the passenger carriages.

Common decency and the doctor in him forced him to stop and render what assistance he could, despite his brain knowing what he would find.

He peered through a rent in the side of the carriage and the scene inside would haunt him for ever.

Instinctively he narrowed his line of sight from the grand scale of destruction to find the nearest body, but without equipment the twisted metal didn't allow his entry and he scanned the faces he could see for any sign of life. Nobody moved, not even a twitch, so he eased back to try the next carriage as a young man appeared at his shoulder.

'This carriage will have to be left for the rescue workers. We can't get in and we'll be more useful to those we can reach.' The young man swallowed and nodded.

A group of half a dozen commuters had arrived

and Stewart directed them to the end carriages. 'Just help the walking wounded. Don't move anyone until the emergency workers arrive. Watch for power lines.'

Stewart closed his eyes and sent a prayer of thanks as a wail of sirens filled the air, assuring him that he wouldn't be in charge of this horror.

He saw tragic events and terrified parents in his paediatric consultancy work but to face this shocking reality made him wish for a nice simple premature twin birth and his team.

He dreaded what he would find in carriage two as he skirted hot metal and clambered towards the opening between the carriages. What he inhaled was smoke, and a fire was the last thing they needed. Given the blasting heat of the day, he should have expected it.

A paramedic, the first of a strong contingent alighting beside the tracks, sprang from his vehicle and touched Stewart's arm. 'I'll take over, sir.'

Stewart glanced at the man in mid-stride but didn't falter. 'I'm a doctor. I've a relative on this train. I'd like to stay.'

When she woke, she could hear the weak cry of a baby as the acrid tendrils of smoke began to fill the carriage.

The infant cried again. A baby? A sudden jolt from her rounded tummy and then a pain squeezed her abdomen rock hard beneath her searching fingers, but she couldn't connect the thoughts. There was something about a baby.

The pain eased and instinctively she looked for the crying infant, but when she tried to move she realised her arm was caught.

She lay on her side under several pieces of luggage and a broken seat with her cheek against the cold glass of the window.

It took a few moments to realise the window lay where the floor had been. The carriage—she must be in a train—resembled a stacked bonfire and something was burning.

Even then fogginess about the sequence of events distanced her from the horror. All her instincts focussed on the baby's cry despite the smoke and the noise of people shouting and the creaking of hot metal.

The woman tried to move her arm but her whole system seemed sluggish. Or maybe she was faint because, apart from a pounding pain in the side of her head, blood squirted impressively under her broken watch. By the size of the increasing pool beside her arm she knew that wasn't normal.

Fuzzily she watched the puddle grow until her thoughts sharpened and slowly she dislodged the broken seat rail where it pinned her wrist. Strangely, it didn't hurt at all. She felt for the deep gash and slid her fingers over the site, wincing at the return of feeling. The urge to lie down, to invite the blackness that hovered at the edge of her mind to settle over her and fall asleep, ached like a suppressed yawn inside her.

With more pressure from her fingers, the rhythmic

pulse of blood slowed to a trickle and somewhere in the fog of her brain she became conscious that if she let go there was a strong chance she would bleed to death. The thickening smoke made her cough and other fears crowded her mind.

Lost for the moment, from time, place of origin or destination, the woman knew she didn't want to die.

There was another reason she had to live but right at that moment she couldn't pin the incentive, just concentrated on the fact that live she would.

The baby cried weakly again and she turned her head. There was someone else who needed her but she had to stop the bleeding from her wrist or she wouldn't be any use.

She threaded the thin pink pashmina from around her neck and thought fuzzily what a pretty colour it was. She wadded one end of the soft fabric and wrapped the other end awkwardly around her wrist and tucked it in as tightly as she could. The blood seeped through but not as fast as she'd expected.

Then she pushed herself upright so she could crawl forward over the wreckage. She winced at the lance of pain from her damaged arm as she began to search for the crying baby.

Low moans and weak cries began to drift from beyond the door of her carriage and a few strong shouts suggested help was on the way.

Her carriage seemed ominously silent but she

couldn't remember how many people had been seated. She hoped the silence was due to the lack of passengers.

'Come on, baby, cry again,' she muttered, glancing around, then almost toppled off a seat that wasn't as balanced as she'd thought it was.

The baby cried weakly again and the woman's arm caught on a small leather backpack with a formula bottle spilling from a rip. She knew the bag belonged to the baby, she couldn't remember why, but it seemed important so she slid the pack over her shoulders and continued her search.

Then she saw her. The baby lay pinned in her pram, seat belt fastened and her frightened little face screwed up. She looked about a year old.

'Well, hello, there, little one. It looks like you had the best seat in the house.' Her voice cracked as the chill of deep coldness encased her.

The baby whimpered and blinked. Her bright blue eyes were damply lashed and the woman smiled when the infant gave a wobbly grin and held out her hands.

The resilience of children, she thought longingly, as she dug for more strength. There was no way she'd be able to lift the carriage seat that trapped the pram but maybe she could ease the baby from the restraint and drag her out.

The difficulty would be to juggle a baby with one arm while she crawled.

She sat back on her heels and fumbled to undo the top two buttons on her shirt. She lifted the hem of her stretchy knitted shirt and struggled to inch the baby inside next to her skin until the infant was tucked tummy to tummy against her body with her little face popping out under the neckline of her shirt. The woman's neck and shoulders ached with the weight but the baby seemed to like it.

When she began to crawl again each movement seemed harder than the last and the weight hanging under her enticed her to lie down and sleep. The infant clung like a small limpet with her frightened whimpers goading her rescuer on.

She crawled clumsily towards the crazily angled steps of the carriage but the smoke became so acrid the steps seemed much further than she'd anticipated. Her strength ebbed as she coughed.

An old lady lay crumpled, eyes open, staring sightlessly past the window. She didn't blink. Her purple hair looked incongruous at an awkward angle. With sudden clarity, she realised the woman was dead.

'I'm sorry,' she mumbled to the woman as she crawled past and the fog thickened inside her head. Blood pulsed from her wrist again and when a man's face appeared above her he seemed to fade in and out of focus.

His eyes were incredibly blue and incredibly kind as he reached towards her with strong arms, and she prayed the baby would be safe now. As she lifted her face to his, she knew she could go to sleep now. He wouldn't let them die.

Relief blossomed until a huge ripping pain burst from low down in her stomach and the fear of what else could be happening made her lift her face to his.

'Save my baby,' she whispered, and then she felt herself lifted from the carriage as if she were a feather.

Stewart had never seen such willpower to live before and he saw plenty of life-and-death struggles in his work.

In that first moment, when she'd hovered on the edge of losing consciousness, the woman's eyes had glowed, fierce with determination as she'd dragged herself across the wreckage of the carriage through the smoke. How she had navigated the carriage while weighed down with a dangling infant and her life seeping away through the blood-soaked material around her wrist, he could only guess. But she had and had still saved enough energy to demand that he save them.

He knew he would be able to recall her expression any time he closed his eyes. Stewart couldn't believe she had survived the carnage. 'Desiree?'

He lifted her in his arms when she collapsed against him and turned to place her gently on the ground behind him.

Her pulse was thready and far too fast from loss of blood. 'She's critical. I need to find her injuries. We'll triage the baby so I can get to the mother.'

He eased the shocked baby from Desiree's shirt and tried not to see the family resemblance as he placed the baby gently beside her mother for assessment.

Time was important and he needed to do this without emotion—and do it quickly.

The infant had no external bleeding, no obvious limb deformity or head injury. Possibly some abdominal tenderness and tautness, he thought as he ran his fingers lightly over the baby's stomach, but nothing immediately life-threatening—unlike the mother.

He passed his niece to a paramedic, who passed her into another waiting pair of hands, then moved to crouch over the unconscious woman.

Stewart rested his fingers on Desiree's throat to feel her carotid pulse. Her heartbeats fluttered frantically beneath his fingers and his own pulse leapt. 'She needs fluids then blood, urgently, or we'll lose her.'

The paramedic had already opened his kit to assemble the equipment while Stewart briefly ran his hands over Desiree's temple and scalp, then quickly down her body, grimacing at the small but unmistakable bulge of her stomach, before clamping his hand around the blood-soaked scarf on her wrist.

Heaven knew what condition the unborn baby would be in.

'This seems to be the only bleeder, but it's arterial, plus a lump on the side of her head.' The paramedic shone a small torch, and with his free hand Stewart lifted heavily lashed eyelids one at a time to allow the man to shine the light into her pupils.

'The reaction is sluggish but present on both sides,' the paramedic said as he taped the intravenous cannula and line into place on Desiree's arm.

'We need to get her transported and transfused.' Stewart reached down and gathered Desiree up in his arms. 'She's dragged herself across a carriage so I doubt I'll do any more damage if I lift her onto the stretcher. Are you able to transport them together?'

'No problem if you take the infant. I'll keep the fluids going.'

As Desiree was transferred into the ambulance Stewart could see that haemorrhagic shock had set in. They hadn't even been able to measure her blood pressure and wouldn't know if she had sustained organ damage from the near exsanguination.

For the moment he just prayed that her heart wouldn't stop with the loss of blood. He willed the rapid spike of her heartbeat to continue across the monitor screen as the sirens screamed and they hurtled towards the hospital.

The premature contractions had well and truly progressed by the time they realised she was in labour.

CHAPTER TWO

THE room swam and it was hard to focus. Distant throbbing in her arm forced her eyes open. A vaguely familiar backpack rested on the shelf opposite and she stared at it until the blurred lines firmed and stopped their dance.

There was something comforting about having that much control of her vision again.

Then she noticed the serene-faced older lady in the wheelchair. The lady knitted sedately with her bright blue eyes fixed like a white-feathered bird watching her young.

'Hello, Desiree. You're awake.' She knitted with incredible speed without reference to the garment.

Desiree? She looked around but there were only two of them in the room. Desiree?

The lady smiled and allowed her words to sink in before explaining. 'I'm Leanore, your mother-in-law. See, I remembered.'

She looked so pleased. 'Stewart said I haven't

met you before, which is such a relief because I don't remember you. It's such a pain when your brain goes, dear.'

Desiree blinked at the word usage and then moistened dry lips and nodded weakly to Leanore. She cast around for a reason to be lying in a bed surrounded by flowers but couldn't find one.

It seemed Leanore wasn't the only one whose mind had gone. 'Where am I?' Fragments of memory and the crawl from the train crash came back. The man's eyes. She remembered the baby's cries.

'Where's the baby?' Desiree's voice cracked and she cleared her throat at the end of the sentence to calm the semi-hysterical note she could hear in her own voice.

Leanore concentrated and then recited as if she'd been coached. 'You're in St Somebody's Hospital, in Sydney.' The lady frowned and then shook her head. 'No. Can't remember the name of the place.' She shrugged and moved on. 'The little girl is fine, Stewart said. I remember that. I'm sure that's what he said. He's just ducked out for a minute and will be right back. Apparently it's a miracle you both survived.'

A sad expression crossed the old woman's face. 'Your little girl is my granddaughter and she looks just like my darling Sean. I remember he is dead. Now, that's one of those things I'd gladly forget.'

A flutter of panic, like a child's balloon caught by the wind, rose in a bubble in Desiree's chest.

'She's a little girl, not *my* little girl.' Desiree began to cast more frantically around in her memory. 'I'm sure she's not my child. I don't think. I don't remember…' Then it struck her. 'Anything!'

The woman's eyes darkened with compassion. 'I know. Horrible, isn't it? My son said you mightn't. Don't worry. At least your mind will all come back. I'm getting dottier by the day.' Leanore chewed her lip, upset at causing distress. 'I'll call my son, shall I?'

The old lady felt for the bulky necklace around her neck and pressed the centre. She tilted her head at Desiree and winked. 'He makes me wear this and I'm not to stand up unless he's here. He's a good son.'

Desiree had no idea what the lady was talking about but she felt as if she'd woken in a farce. Who was her wheelchair companion and what kind of place was this?

A train crash? She remembered the baby but surely it wasn't her baby? She didn't have a baby. Or did she? Perhaps somewhere in the past she may have been pregnant.

Frantically her eyes darted around the room as she tried to force memories that wouldn't come. Who was she? How could she have had a baby if she didn't remember? How long had she been here?

The blankness of the past rose like nausea in her throat and crowded her already crowded mind until it was all too much. The room swirled as her eyes closed and with relief she allowed the room to fade away until she floated like a balloon again.

'The lady was awake but she didn't know me.' The voices were distant but she couldn't respond.

'She will remember, Mother. You'll have to wait a little longer to be a mother-in-law. Desiree lost a lot of blood.' The man's voice was gentle, as if he found the whole scenario disturbing, and there was something about his compassionate tone that cut through the airiness in her brain and grounded her again.

She opened her eyes reluctantly. The owner of the voice was tall and dark-haired with kind eyes. She registered that his eyes were as blue as his mother's and there was something reassuringly familiar about his strong face.

The brightness of his doctor's white coat made her blink.

Stewart Kramer stared intently at the ghostly pale woman lying back on the pillows. It was a miracle she had lived, he thought. Dark smudges lay under her eyes and her bruised cheek was swollen and purple from the accident.

She confused him. Desiree didn't have that flashy racehorse quality about her that had consistently seemed Sean's type and her obviously fierce will would not have sat comfortably with Sean's need to dominate.

This woman had curves in abundance and her dark waves of hair lay softly against her cheek. Maybe Sean had acquired a more genuine taste in women because there was a lot about Desiree that made Stewart think more of wholesome warmth and strength of character than fashion magazines and the fast lane.

Desiree's grey eyes glistened with tears but she blinked them away as he watched her grapple with her situation. Inexplicably Stewart had to fight against the urge to scoop her up and cradle her head on his shoulder.

No doubt the urge would be to do with the horror of when he'd first seen her surrounded by those who had died and the gritty hold she'd maintained on her life despite her massive blood loss.

Desiree eased higher in the bed and closed her eyes briefly, and Stewart presumed she felt light-headed.

'You seem vaguely familiar,' she said in a soft voice. 'Maybe you know the answers to some of my questions?'

Stewart tried to imagine what it would feel like to wake up after such an event.

His mother, with her illness, lived in confusion every day to some degree, and he thanked God for her unfailing good humour. He didn't fancy the idea for himself. 'I'll try, but I'm a paediatrician here, not your doctor.'

She looked at him with those big silver-grey eyes, eyes shadowed with pain and bewilderment, and a sudden twist of jealous rage against his careless brother stunned him with the raw emotion. It wasn't Sean's fault the train had crashed so his sentiment didn't make sense.

It was just that she seemed so different to what he'd imagined Sean's wife would be like. Sean had never cared for real people. What the hell had she been doing with Sean? He wanted to throttle the truth out of his brother but it was too late now. So too was being unexpectedly affected by meeting Desiree.

He ground his teeth and forced the useless emotions back into a deep cave in his chest and sealed the door. When he spoke his voice sounded coldly clinical, even to his own ears. 'You have amnesia, probably retrograde, involving memory from the time prior to the blow to your head.'

'When will I remember?' Her voice shook, and with compunction he reached out and covered her fingers. Her hand was soft and defenceless under his.

'In the accident you were knocked unconscious for a short time. Goodness knows what you hit on impact. With the swelling near your brain your memory could take hours to return or even months.'

She watched him as if he had all the answers and Stewart felt inadequate for the first time in a very long time.

'Will my memory definitely come back?' she asked, and he felt the weight of her need as if it were his obligation to make her world right.

That was the rub. 'In the majority of amnesia cases, most of the patient's memory does come back in time.'

'So reassuring,' she murmured ironically, and turned her head away from him on the pillow. Strangely, she left her fingers curled safe in his, though. Stewart found himself absurdly touched by her trust.

He left the silence between them and it built until she turned back to face him. There was resolution on her face that he could only admire and the urge to comfort her returned with force. What was it about this woman that made it so easy to read her thoughts? What was it about her that made him *want* to read them? The concept elbowed for room in his own crowded mind.

She cleared her throat. 'So you can tell me anything you like and I have to believe you until my memory returns?' she said.

He had to applaud her dry sense of humour because he doubted he'd be up to jokes in Desiree's position.

He glanced at Leanore and his mother stared vaguely out the window, sidetracked in confusion caused by her tumour. He did it for Leanore every day.

At least he was practised at orientating lost people. 'So it appears. You will just have to sue me for any incorrect answers.'

Desiree had no choice but to trust him for the moment. She steeled herself for the question she dreaded the answer to. 'Who is Desiree?'

Obviously this was not the question he'd expected, by the lift of his dark brows. Well, it was the one she needed an answer to the most, and she held her breath as she waited.

'You.' He'd said it gently but the answer still

slammed into her. 'Your name is Desiree Kramer.'
She winced as she exhaled.

She'd been afraid of that. Desiree Kramer? No
bells rang, no recognition sparked. So it was true. She
couldn't even remember her own name.

He enunciated slowly, as if she were a slow learner.
'Desiree Kramer, lately of Queensland, and newly
arrived in Sydney.'

Desiree screwed her nose up and shook her head.
'And you are sure my name is Desiree? Not something simpler or plainer?'

'Desiree, I'm afraid, but we could call you anything
you like if that would make you more comfortable.'

'Don't patronise me.' She sighed and accepted
what she had been afraid of. It was incredibly hard,
not having a past to call on.

'I'm sorry,' he said. 'That was not my intention.'

She gathered her frayed composure around her.
'I'm sorry for snapping. Do I know you?' Her voice
had wearied, and she'd closed her eyes again.

'I'm your brother-in-law. Stewart Kramer.'

Startled, her eyes flew open. 'I have a sister?' She
didn't remember that!

'You married my brother. I don't know your family.'

She shook her head at this new information and
her whole body stiffened in the bed. No way. 'I'm
not married.'

'No.' Stewart agreed. 'You are a widow with a
twelve-month-old child.'

She barely heard his second pronouncement because the first one had blown her away. 'I mean,' Desiree enunciated slowly and clearly, 'I have never been married.'

Stewart shrugged slightly. For some reason his voice had cooled and she wondered if it had been her or his brother that had annoyed him. This was all too much but he had more to share and he was her only link to reality.

She tried to concentrate as he went on when all she wanted to do was sleep.

'You married last April. Your husband, my brother, died in a car accident on New Year's Day, eight weeks ago.'

Now she was a widow? Her heart was turning somersaults in her chest and she felt sick. 'There's no memory of anything beyond waking up a short time ago.' She fought against rising panic and stared around the walls of the room, as if the secret of her lost life could be found there.

She felt abandoned, confused, and at the mercy of these people she didn't recognise. She heard the shake in her voice but there was nothing she could do about it because she was doing well to avoid lapsing into hysterics.

She shook her head and then grimaced at the discomfort. Maybe she should worry about all this later. She didn't think she could do it now. 'Whatever. I can't remember anything. My head hurts.'

She shut her eyes and then opened them again. This had to be a big mistake. 'Do I know you well? Are you sure you're right?'

She hadn't fazed him. How could he be so calm when her whole past life had disappeared? His voice was even and unruffled as he went on. 'Except for the accident, we've never met. Your identification was in the backpack.'

She glanced at the bag on the shelf again. 'How do you know it's my backpack?'

'It was on your back when I found you.'

'You were there?'

She nodded and then stared at him. His kind blue eyes kindled a flame of recognition and a strange feeling of comfort and safety finally seeped into her.

He was a good man. She felt it, so she supposed she'd have to believe him and trust in his word. As she looked into his eyes, a strange, deeper recognition began to shimmer between them, and she couldn't look away.

She remembered. He had been there in the wreckage. 'So it was you and not a dream.'

He cleared his throat and his hand tightened on hers. 'It's a miracle you can remember anything. The scene was chaotic.'

'I don't remember much, but I remember…' Her eyes widened and she remembered the pain in her stomach. Her voice dropped to a whisper as the ache of realisation hit her. Her baby. 'I was pregnant!'

She pulled her hand out of his hold and slid her fingers slowly under the covers to her flat stomach. It was then she felt the loss of her baby within. Her rounded stomach had gone, replaced by emptiness, and she hadn't been awake to know.

Her hand returned above the sheets and searched for his. 'Did I lose my baby?'

'No.' He let that answer seep in slowly.

Desiree didn't understand. 'What month is this?' She swallowed the ball of fear and grief in her throat and prepared herself for the worst. Tears pricked her eyes as she sucked in her flat stomach. My poor baby.

With her fingers clutched around his, a small measure of comfort warmed the sudden coldness of her soul.

'No, your baby is alive but it is the twenty-sixth of February, so she has some growing to do,' he said.

She paused before she looked at him again, afraid that if she saw his face he would retract that tiny hope she'd heard him correctly.

His fingers tightened their grip on her hand. 'After the accident you went into premature labour. We didn't know you were in labour until just before she was born.'

Desiree remembered the pain in stomach. 'You said she. I had a girl?'

'We estimate your daughter was born eleven weeks early but she is stable at the moment. She will need to stay in a large hospital like this one, if all goes well, for the next few months. She's in our neonatal intensive care two floors down.'

Her daughter was alive. There was hope. 'Eleven weeks is very early. I'm sure of that.'

'Your daughter is breathing for herself and seems to be adapting to the outside world well, considering she wasn't ready for us—and you had lost a lot of blood. She weighed just over a kilogram and is a fighter.'

He smiled and Desiree remembered his eyes again from the train crash. How could she remember that and not her own name? But there was something infinitely reassuring about sharing that one memory at least.

'Your daughter has already shown she has the will to survive, like her mother.' There was no mistaking he admired her baby for that. 'And she is in the next best place to grow.'

Desiree's heart pounded. She had a baby daughter. 'When can I see her?'

He produced a digital print of a tiny baby in a humidicrib and passed it over to her. A thin red-faced skinned rabbit looked back at her.

A lost baby, a lost pregnancy, a baby she would have dreamed of meeting in a wondrous birth surrounded by people who loved her. Too many losses to cope with. Tears welled as she thought of her daughter alone, in a crib, and she couldn't be with her. 'When…?'

'Perhaps you can see her this evening. You've only just regained consciousness. I'm not your doctor, but he'd agree it's too soon to go riding around the hospital, even in a wheelchair.'

She sagged back. Even that small exertion had tired her.

'We are taking good care of your daughter and she is stable at the moment.'

She could hardly believe her pregnancy was over before it had even been remembered.

Then he said something even more frightening. 'It worries me you haven't asked about your other child.'

Desiree watched his lips move but the words seem to come from a long way off as she wondered what her tiny daughter looked like.

He spoke again. 'Do you remember I said you were a widow with another child? You have a twelve-month-old. Shall we bring Sophie to you? They have her down in the children's ward for observation.'

She tore her thoughts away from the picture of her tiny baby and looked at him blankly.

He explained again. 'Your other daughter? You told me to keep her safe when we first met.'

The other baby? What else had she forgotten? Had another child been mentioned? Perhaps. 'You may have said that before but I don't remember.'

Desiree frowned as she tried to remember. She had heard a baby crying in the wreckage. Had that baby been hers? 'I heard her cry.'

How could she not recall her own flesh and blood? Was that possible? It didn't make senses. What if it was a mistake, or a conspiracy, or a bad dream? 'I wish I remembered.'

The first of his revelations rose to stun her again. 'I can't believe I was married and don't remember.'

Stewart grimaced at what a marriage it would have been, unless Sean had changed a lot. He watched her struggle with all the information and worried that he'd burdened her with too much, too soon.

She tilted her head towards him and her grey eyes seemed to peer inside his soul as she sought answers.

He blinked and looked away, not sure what had just passed between them and not willing to pursue the thought. This was fanciful imagining and unlike him.

He fought against a sudden stirring of emotion he hadn't allowed himself to feel for many years. Especially when he looked down at her fingers as they disappeared inside his bigger hand. He wondered why she had decided not to wear her wedding ring.

Something had shifted, something that shouldn't have shifted with this woman who was related by law, and who was the last woman he wanted to be attracted to. There was nothing he could do about that now except ignore any such emotion and help her as much as he could.

Stewart glanced across at his mother, sitting patiently against the wall as she knitted. She had the glazed look of sudden tiredness she seemed to feel more often. He'd been a fool to bring her but she'd so wanted to be here when Desiree woke up.

He never knew when Leanore would lapse into one of those turns that kept her in bed for days and she deserved to at least meet her daughter-in-law.

There were so many ways his mind wanted to go but he could only do one thing at a time. 'We'll go now, Mother.'

Leanore blinked and looked at him brightly, and he knew she had lost her space in time for the moment. 'Where will we go?'

'Home, darling. Desiree is tired.'

Leanore creased her brow. 'Desiree who?'

Stewart sighed and squeezed his mother's shoulder gently. 'We'll leave Desiree to rest for a while and see Children's Ward about bringing your granddaughter up here after she wakes up.' He saw the moment her memory returned and he smiled as his mother nodded.

He looked at Desiree, her eyes now drooping with fatigue. 'Sleep now. We'll bring Sophie to you later this afternoon. After tea I'll take you to the neonatal intensive care, or NICU as they call it, to see your new daughter, if it is all right with your doctor.'

Desiree nodded tiredly but there was one thing she had to do. 'Before you leave, would you pass the backpack, please?'

'We'll see you later, Desiree.' Stewart laid the backpack gently in her lap and then turned his mother's wheelchair towards the door.

'Later,' he said, and she closed her eyes as they left the room.

Desiree's head ached quietly but the pain was overshadowed by the enormity of losing who she was and what was in her past.

Lost memories of a twelve-month-old baby and dead husband and now the reality that she risked losing a baby she only fuzzily remembered being pregnant with. It was all too much.

It was a nightmare and surely she would wake up soon.

CHAPTER THREE

SHE didn't feel like a Desiree. She felt like a Jane or a Mary. They were safe, kind, reassuring names. You'd have to be exotic to be called Desiree and she didn't feel exotic. But maybe that was the knock on the head too. Maybe she'd shortened her name to something easy or used her middle name?

She must ask Stewart if she had a middle name.

Desiree looked around the sterile hospital room. The walls were pale green, a soothing colour, but she didn't feel soothed. The bed was electric and the furniture wooden, not metal, but there was nothing homey or reassuring to help her state of mind, except the flowers from a woman she didn't know.

Her hand fell to the soft kid of the backpack on her lap and she frowned at the chic but drab leather.

She couldn't imagine choosing it. Maybe the bag had been a gift from her husband. A man she couldn't remember, and therefore couldn't mourn.

A man living estranged from his family if some of Stewart's comments were anything to go by.

Inside, an eye-make-up pack revealed a mirror and she flicked it open to stare into the tiny frame to see her face.

A stranger looked back. A very pale stranger who looked more like a plain Jane then a Desiree! Grey eyes, ordinary-looking mouth and nose, with an extraordinary bruise on one cheek. Dark mop of hair with blood congealed in the fringe. Not a good look and hardly reassuring. She snapped the mirror shut and pushed it down to the bottom of the bag as if to erase what she'd just seen.

Desiree pulled a soft leather wallet from the satchel and unclipped it.

Loose change and no paper money at all? That seemed strange. No driver's licence—maybe she didn't drive. A collection of gold and platinum credit cards all in the name of Mrs Desiree Kramer, a health card and a private health insurance card. A train ticket to Sydney—lot of good that had done her.

One sleeve of the wallet held a photo of a baby, obviously her unremembered daughter, Sophie. Tears welled. How could she have forgotten her own baby?

'I'm sorry I don't remember you, Sophie,' she said to the photo.

She ran her fingers over her stomach and desolation hit her again. Except for the slight softness that could have been recently stretched skin, she couldn't tell she'd been pregnant.

Perhaps she hadn't shown much at nearly seven months. What sort of pregnancy had it been? Had she been sick or well? Excited to be having another baby or too sad after the loss of her husband to be in tune with her foetus?

Instinctively she touched her breasts and both felt tender. She guessed she'd figure out the breastfeeding as she went along, even though there would be no poster-perfect pictures of her new babe at the breast for a long time to come. Hopefully she'd breastfed Sophie and it would come back to her.

She guessed there might be many weeks before her baby would be strong enough to feed normally.

Desiree shook her head in despair. How did she accept that she was a widow of a man she couldn't remember? Or the mother of a child in the paediatric ward? Plus the dreadful knowledge that her premature baby was fighting for her life on another floor?

All this when she hadn't even recognised her own name—it was too much. She dragged her hands over her eyes and squeezed her fingers into her eye sockets, as though the pressure would bring back visions from her past life.

All it did was increase her headache and circulate stars.

Her fingers fell to pluck at the bag again. 'I don't feel like Desiree Kramer,' she said, out loud this time, and the horror of having no memories to anchor in reality burst in her chest like a cave full of bats exploding from their perches.

Panic fluttered with larger and larger wings until she thought her throat would close.

Desiree fought the emotion as she clutched the bag tightly between her fingers. She breathed in and out grimly until she'd fought down the panic.

You'll be fine. You'll be fine, she told herself. Everything would work out—and whether it was the white coat or the kind eyes, she did trust Stewart, her new brother-in-law.

She trusted the sweetness in the face of the obviously forgetful Leanore.

Most importantly, she and both her daughters had survived.

Four hours later, Desiree's new mother-in-law, pushed in her wheelchair by Stewart, returned with a nurse who steered a portable cot into the room.

A little girl stood clutching the rails with her tiny feet planted determinedly into the mattress as she swayed with the movement. Enormous blue eyes stared tremulously at the grown-ups.

Desiree's eldest daughter looked chubby and alert but decidedly lost. Why wouldn't she feel lost? Her own mother couldn't remember her!

When the nurse lifted Sophie and placed her on the bed beside her, Desiree had to admit she felt better with the weight and feel of the little body against her. She gathered Sophie into her arms and hugged her.

Sophie had eyes like her uncle's and grandmother's. She stared up at Desiree, and then her little face dimpled and she grinned toothily. Unconsciously, Desiree hugged her close again.

'Well, that's the first smile we've seen the wee thing give since she came in.' The nurse nodded complacently at the picture in front of her.

Leanore smiled mistily and Stewart lifted one sardonic eyebrow. 'Well, Sophie remembers you.'

'I wish I remembered her.' Desiree spoke softly and brushed the baby's cheek with wondering fingers. Her daughter's skin was downy soft and far too pale.

The children's ward nurse bustled forward. 'She won't drink for us. I've brought a bottle up with me. Maybe she'll take some milk from you.'

Desiree stared down into the bright little eyes. Sophie? She tried the name out. No bells rang, nothing about the little face or her name was familiar, but Desiree couldn't doubt that she was at ease with the toddler.

Sophie latched onto the teat immediately and Desiree smiled as she looked down into the trusting face below her as the level of milk in the bottle rapidly receded towards the teat. At least she could do something right for her daughter. 'I'm sorry, Sophie. I have forgotten you for the moment, but I'll look after you.'

'And we'll look after you.' Leanore rubbed her hands with delight at the picture in front of her. She turned to her son. 'They will come home to us? Won't they, Stewart?'

'Of course.' There were unexpected misgivings in his tone and Desiree shot him a glance.

Something was bothering him and Desiree didn't welcome the added stress of wondering what his problem was. The last thing she needed was another undercurrent she didn't understand.

'I'm sure I will be able to look after my daughters and myself quite well without your help.' She hoped the pure bravado didn't show.

He shook his head decisively. 'You'll have enough on your plate, travelling to Neonatal each day. You'll need help and we'll give it to you.'

His voice was flat. 'You moved here to live with us. I'm sure even Sean would agree to you accepting our help especially now.' He included his mother in a glance. 'We're glad to finally have the opportunity to meet you and Sophie.'

'We live quite close to the hospital and have plenty of room. Stay at least until we're sure you won't suffer any other health setbacks. You could stay longer, of course.'

He produced a final inducement. 'It would be easier for Sophie if she didn't have to come to the NICU all the time with you.'

She couldn't dispute any of his rationales, or an

identity she couldn't remember. It just didn't feel right to lean on them so heavily.

Stewart went on. 'Remember that Leanore is Sophie's grandmother and she has been denied access since her granddaughter's birth.'

'What do you mean, denied?' Desiree frowned at the censure in his voice. Had she prevented Leanore seeing her granddaughter? Had her husband—and she had let him? She didn't like Stewart's tone or the inference she had hurt his mother.

He avoided a direct answer and softened his tone. 'My mother wants to get to know her grandchild.' Suddenly it was Leanore who wanted to look after them, which was at odds with his caring eyes. Desiree wondered if he had reservations for another reason.

Why had he changed?

She removed the empty bottle from her daughter's mouth and sat her up to burp her again. Sophie blew a bubble at her and Desiree kissed her cheek. Thank goodness her daughter was too young to know she had been forgotten by her own mother.

Desiree's eyes narrowed with the effort of pinpointing her greatest concern, but she was interrupted by Sophie's wind.

They all smiled at the third loud burp but despite the surface amusement something wasn't right. Not just in this room but with her whole world.

So many things were out of kilter she had no way of diagnosing the most worrying feature.

It was too exhausting to worry about things she couldn't change for the moment, so she rested back and just savoured the weight of Sophie in her arms. Her head ached.

Later that evening Stewart pushed Desiree's wheelchair into the neonatal intensive care unit, and strangely Desiree felt less adrift than she had since she'd woken up.

She was so terrified for her baby but not overwhelmed by Neonatal Intensive Care, which was strange.

The beep and hum of the equipment, the bustle of medical and nursing staff, the parents beside most cribs and the tiny patients in their plastic cocoons and open cots all seemed to make sense. Maybe she'd been in one of these places before.

Then again it could have been because Stewart was there. He was so solid and concerned, uncomfortably attractive, but she was trying to ignore that with all she had on her plate, but most of all he seemed so patiently kind.

'It's a pretty daunting place,' said Stewart as he nodded to a nurse, 'but, believe me, you will get used to it.'

Desiree allowed his words to wash over her as she glanced around. She wasn't daunted by the place, just that her daughter was here, and she wondered about that. Was it because she'd just been in a train crash? Had her senses been so overloaded by new situations that she was immune for the moment?

At least in this unit there was ordered chaos and Stewart was the boss. She had some control with her access to him.

She obeyed the sign and washed her hands. Almost as if she knew where her daughter was, she looked ahead to the furthermost cribs, home to the most critical patients. Stewart pushed the wheelchair forward.

'She's up this way,' Stewart said, as they passed alcoves of four cribs at a time, each bay seeming to utilise more equipment than the last. Some babies were tiny, some less so, and some were in ordinary Perspex cots.

Desiree's daughter lay tiny and exposed, her red shiny skin translucent, her miniature hands smaller than the top of her mother's finger and her bald head smaller than Desiree's palm.

The reality of her daughter's struggle hit her. Her baby should be safe within her uterus, not exposed to pain and fear in the bright lights, fluctuating temperatures and noise of a neonatal nursery.

Desiree felt tears well into her eyes and she swallowed to clear the lump from her throat. 'She's so fragile. So beautiful,' she said in a whisper.

Stewart smiled warmly at the crib and then at Desiree. 'She is very beautiful. I'm glad you think that. A lot of people can't see the beauty in a premature baby. They look so different to the image most people have of newborn babies.' He shook his head at the unenlightened. 'She is a miracle of creation.'

Stewart crouched down and slipped his arm around Desiree's shoulder and hugged her gently as they peered into the crib.

Somehow Desiree knew he would do that for any new mother confronted by a tiny skinned rabbit of a baby, but she was glad of even that small comfort. More than glad—she was in desperate need of strong arms around her.

'She's gorgeous,' he went on. 'Her skin is only a few cells thick and very delicate. Her tiny veins are so clear under her skin the vessels look like lace. At the moment we're using the umbilical vein for intravenous access, which is what the contraption stuck to her tummy is about.'

There was an ice-cream-stick bridge of balsa and strapping taped to her baby's soft belly that supported a long tube connected to the IV stand and fluids.

He pointed to the thicker red tubing that sealed each of Desiree's daughter's tiny nostrils. 'She's managing well on CPAP, which is the name we give this nasal continuous positive airway pressure that keeps her lungs inflated.'

He checked to see that she was following his explanation. 'A tiny amount of air stays in the lungs to stop the lung surfaces sticking together like wet paper.

'Whenever she doesn't breathe, the machine

breathes for her, as necessary. But she's doing most of it herself.'

They both looked at the diminutive face disfigured by the thick tubing.

Stewart lowered his voice. 'I know the tubing does stretch her nostrils and make them look larger than they are but there are disadvantages for throat intubation of infants as well.'

Desiree found herself checking the monitors and glancing over the intravenous fluids and she felt reassured by the numbers. She still had trouble grasping that this was her baby connected to these leads and monitors, but surely 'reassured' seemed a strange thing to be in the circumstances.

Had she been here or somewhere like this before?

Had Sophie been born prematurely as well? Could she be as familiar with this equipment as it all seemed?

Her heart pounded with the thrill of excitement at the thought of a breakthrough in her memory block.

Surely most parents wouldn't feel this comfortable with such a bombardment of technology around their tiny precious baby. She must have loads of experience with such a place or been there before.

Stewart broke into her thoughts as he introduced a third person. 'This is Gina. Gina is one of your daughter's primary carers. She's a neonatal nurse.'

'Hello, Gina.' Desiree forced herself to smile at the tall girl who was caring for her daughter and tried not to think she looked as if she should still be at school.

The young nurse stood up from her stool beside the crib where she'd been recording observations and shook Desiree's hand.

Gina grinned at Desiree. 'Your daughter has a very determined will. Dr Kramer says she takes after her mother.'

Desiree smiled and glanced at Stewart before looking back at her daughter. It warmed her that he thought that and it had been good of him to say so. .

She still couldn't believe her baby was here to see in front of her eyes when she could barely remember her pregnancy. 'Can I touch her?'

Stewart answered. 'Absolutely. But remember if you touch her charts, or a phone, or anything, you need to wash your hands before you open the door again. The humidicribs are perfect places for germs to grow and she's very susceptible at the moment.'

Desiree nodded and gently opened the crib door and stroked the top of her daughter's tiny hand. 'She's so tiny but perfect.'

'I think so,' Stewart agreed, and there was no doubting his sincerity.

Desiree knew her daughter was in good hands. 'So what have you done for her so far?'

Stewart glanced at Gina. 'Very determined.'

He looked back at Desiree with a smile. 'Are you ready for this?'

Desiree glanced at her baby. She had to be. 'Yes.'

Stewart nodded. 'OK. She has respiratory distress

syndrome because of her tiny lungs and her sudden arrival but we are treating that with the CPAP I mentioned earlier.

'Her lungs did not have enough of a substance called surfactant in the air spaces. We gave her a dose of surfactant when she came down to us and that helps the stiffness of her immature lungs so she can inflate them and maintain the expansion she needs to breathe.'

Desiree nodded. That was clear so far. 'So how long will she stay on CPAP?'

'Only a few days or possibly more than a week, depending on how much help she needs.' Stewart glanced at the oxygen saturation monitor screen and nodded at the reading. 'The amount of oxygen present in your daughter's skin at the moment is ninety seven per cent, which is great. We don't need one hundred per cent and would prefer your baby's levels stay a little under that because of the risk of damage to her eyes.'

Desiree didn't want to think about damage to eyes. 'What about infections? What if she does get one? You said she is at risk.'

'Your daughter is having forty-eight hours of antibiotics intravenously for the risk of infection from her birth. Her skin swab cultures have been clear so far and that medication should stop tomorrow.'

She would pray that everyone washed their hands properly. She could feel herself becoming paranoid already. Was this what premature babies did to you?

She tried to think of something to divert her mind away from the image of other people's dirty hands going near her daughter and germs colonising happily in the crib. 'What about food?'

'The fluids that are dripping into her umbilical vein keep her hydrated and with enough glucose for energy. Gina will discuss tiny tube feeds of breast milk a little later with you.'

Desiree felt absurd relief. Finally something she could do for her daughter that no one else could.

Stewart stood up. 'The last thing for the moment is that your daughter has mild anaemia. She will probably need a blood transfusion to increase the red cells in her blood, but I'll check with you again before we consider that. Anaemia is fairly common in premature infants.'

Stewart pointed to the crisp white hospital card with 'Baby of Desiree Kramer' written in black pen. 'Now you will have to think about names for your daughter.'

There it was again, only this time in black and white. Desiree frowned, unable to come to terms with the unfamiliarity of her own name, and then she shook her head to concentrate on Stewart's question.

To her surprise, she had no trouble choosing her daughter's name because it floated into her head unbidden.

'Her name is Simone Louise. The name feels right and not having her named seems so cold and unfeeling when I can't even remember her birth.'

'Simone Louise is a beautiful name,' Stewart said quietly.

Another neonatal nurse signalled from further down the unit and he nodded back. 'I have to leave you with Gina for a while but I'll come back to collect you or arrange for someone else to get you back to your bed.'

He was leaving her? How would she cope without him there? Even in this short time she was used to his calming presence. She steeled herself to smile. 'I'll be fine. Thank you for your explanations, Stewart.'

He patted her shoulder and she fancied, he moved off almost reluctantly. She watched his tall figure move commandingly down the unit and he drew attention without effort. Surely his brother had been like him and that would explain why she had married. But not how she could forget.

'He has been very kind,' Desiree said to Gina, and Gina watched Stewart's broad shoulders as he moved away.

'He is the best paediatrician I have ever worked with. We all appreciate the way he communicates with the parents and the staff. It makes him very easy to work in his team. She grinned. 'Plus he's easy to look at.'

Gina blushed and then turned back to Simone and became professional again. 'So you have named her, then. Simone Louise it is.' Gina wrote Simone's name on the baby card and then put the pen down.

She pulled her stool closer to the wheelchair. 'Dr

Kramer mentioned feeding Simone. How were you planning to feed your baby?'

'Breast.' Desiree had that clear at least.

'Great,' said Gina. 'They've found if premature babies are given even a mil or two of expressed breast milk from their mother it helps prevent the intestinal problems that have been so devastating in the past and still are sometimes.

'NEC, or necrotising enterocolitis, is an inflammation of the bowel wall which causes a swollen stomach and is very dangerous for preterm infants. The condition is less common if babies are breastfed.'

That knowledge resonated for Desiree. 'I remember that from somewhere but I haven't figured it out yet.' Perhaps a clue to her past? she thought. 'I guess there will be a lot of those times until I remember.'

'Probably.' Gina didn't say much but her look was warmly sympathetic and it was obvious that Stewart had forewarned her about Desiree's amnesia. It made Desiree feel better that Gina didn't think she was mad just because she'd lost her memory.

'Anyway…' They were talking about her daughter here, not amnesia. 'I'll gladly leave some colostrum for her before I go back to the ward this afternoon.'

'Great. I'll take whatever you get, maybe half a mil or more, and pop it down a tiny tube into her tummy when Dr Kramer says it's OK.'

Gina elaborated. 'We've found the benefit so dramatic that all our extremely premature babies, without exception, are given what begins as tiny amounts of expressed breast milk at least for the first month, even if the mother is planning to artificially feed later on.'

Desiree nodded. 'Of course. It is a real break-through. At least there is something I can do for her.' Suddenly her head swam and nausea began to build. 'I'm afraid I'll have to go and lie down.'

Gina took one look at her and scurried off. 'You do need your bed.'

Exhaustion pounded Desiree in waves but she was immensely reassured by her daughter's condi-tion, Gina's competence and Stewart's skill as a pae-diatrician.

She scanned the long room and allowed the sights and noises of the intensive care nursery to soak into her subconscious to distract her from the waves of nausea while she waited for Gina to arrange her transfer back to the ward.

She heard the hiss of the ventilators, the ticking of the intravenous monitors and the electronic beeping of twenty tiny heartbeats.

Movement was constant. Neonatal nurses glided between the cribs, reading monitors, recording obser-vations, straightening a tiny body that had become skewed diagonally across a miniature mattress.

Brow-creased parents hovered anxiously as they peered into their baby's space—too frightened to put their hands inside the Perspex cages to touch the fragile and translucent creature that held their future dreams.

The blue glow around several cribs came from the phototherapy lights. She knew that the exposure of a baby's naked skin to the special lights would help the breakdown the extra bilirubin their tiny livers couldn't cope with.

She knew that neonatal jaundice caused babies' skins to become yellow and, if severe, babies, and especially premature babies, were at risk of brain damage, apart from becoming too sleepy to feed.

She glanced back at Simone and reminded herself to ask what her daughter's bilirubin level was. She shook her head decisively. Obviously she had some previous knowledge or experience with premature babies. When had Desiree Kramer got that?

The alarm connected to Simone beeped and Desiree narrowed her eyes to watch her daughter's chest.

Desiree wanted to lunge across and open the door to the crib and nudge her daughter into movement but they were monitoring Simone's need for stimulation. The CPAP clicked in and her tiny chest rose and fell with the machine.

As Simone's heart rate picked up so Desiree's slowed down.

She didn't care if she knew this stuff. Watching your own child dependent on machinery to live was harrowing and horrific and she felt the loneliest person in the world.

She didn't even have people from her past to comfort her. Her whole life had started today, and if she wasn't Desiree Kramer, then, except for this tiny human being opposite her and Sophie, she was totally alone.

Desiree watched Stewart stride towards her. She needed to know if Stewart was really a part of her life or not. If he wasn't, she needed to know the truth as soon as possible.

Desiree glanced at the card with her baby's name and then her own name underneath.

Simone felt right, Sophie fitted comfortably, the neonatal unit she could cope with, but everything else felt wrong.

CHAPTER FOUR

BACK in her room, Desiree sank into bed and stared tiredly at the backpack on the shelf. The nausea had settled slightly when she'd lifted her feet up onto the bed. Stewart had left to return the wheelchair but he was coming back. They needed to talk so she hoped he had the time to spare her.

The more Desiree stared at the backpack the less she believed she was Desiree Kramer. And if she wasn't that woman, who was she? And where was Desiree?'

'What's wrong?' Stewart asked the question quietly as soon as he entered the room, and she looked up at him.

Her protector, because that's what he'd been, her rock in a sea of confusion. He was a tall man, strong featured and handsome with an air of authority without arrogance that encouraged reassurance.

She'd avoided thinking about the magnetism in those intense blue eyes or the inkling they held more than kindness because it would be dangerous to go there.

Unless she wasn't really a widow.

Desiree took a deep breath. What she was going to say could alienate him and leave her alone again. But it had to be said. And there was danger in relying on this man too much. She felt the truth of that at a time when she didn't know many other truths.

'I believe I'm not Desiree Kramer.' Desiree searched his face for a reaction to her words but his expression didn't change.

Stewart sank into the chair as if she'd just asked about the weather. 'I think you are Desiree.' He said simply. 'There are too many correlations.'

'Coincidences happen.' She tried to sound reasonable and not pitifully stubborn.

Stewart lifted his shoulders as if to say he would hear her out. 'All right. Let's run through them.'

He ticked them off on his fingers. 'I was to meet that particular train, that number carriage, and pick up my sister-in-law whom I have never met and her one-year-old baby.'

Desiree shrugged. She had no idea what his agenda had been.

Stewart went on. 'The woman I was to meet was twenty-six years old, seven months pregnant, and travelling alone, except for her baby. I checked later and they found no one else in the carriage who

matched that description. You were found unconscious, amnesic and with Sophie and Desiree's bag.'

Desiree sighed. 'Did you have a photo? Do I look
like you imagined? Tell me about Desiree. What
did…?' Desiree paused. 'I do? Where did I live?'

His shoulders lifted. 'We knew very little about
you. I believe you were an actress before you married. Your husband and I had a major falling out two
years before he died, and his revenge was estranging
himself and his family from my mother.

'Sean liked fast cars, beautiful women and contact
sports. He was quick-tempered and always in brawls.
I could never understand his desire for that. There are
ways to settle disputes other than by assaulting
someone in the heat of the moment.'

Desiree frowned. Sean didn't sound like the sort
of man who would have attracted her, but she said
nothing as Stewart went on.

'Sean knew our mother was ill. He knew I would
go to any lengths to protect her from distress when I
could. He considered her my weakness. I will do anything to make her happy and make up for the pain
Sean caused her. Sean had no compunction in exploit-
ing that.'

Desiree wondered at the harshness in his voice.
It seemed out of character for the man she had come
to rely on. 'You don't sound enamoured of your
late brother.'

Stewart looked out the window. 'I regret he died.

His loss was futile and he could have been so much more for my mother's sake, but there was a side to him that concerned me greatly.' He shook his head as if to evade painful memories. 'I don't know. Maybe we would have got on one day. It's too late now.

'I'm still repairing damage he caused—which is ironic, as he was several years older than me.' Stewart visibly shook the memories off.

Desiree raised her eyebrows and smiled to take the sting out of the question. 'Now the damage includes Sophie, Simone and me?'

'I'm sorry.' He leant forward in the chair. 'But let me say now, you, Sophie and Simone may prove to be the best thing my brother has ever done for our family. The three of you are just what my mother needs right now.'

He sat back. 'But I forget that he was your husband and you must have loved him.'

It was Desiree's turn to shake her head. 'I can't recognise his name or remember what he looked like,' she said quietly.

Stewart sighed. 'Of course.' He looked out the window as if he found his next comment difficult. 'Sean and I were uncannily alike in physical appearance but nothing alike in nature. That amused him while I found our looks one of the least amusing facets of our bizarre relationship.' Stewart spoke dryly but didn't elaborate.

'And your mother had no photos of his wedding?'

'Your wedding.' Stewart gently added.

'So you say.' Desiree refused to let this lead go but Stewart shook his head.

'Or photos of Sophie's birth or any news for the two years before he died?' Desiree couldn't believe that she would have estranged her mother-in-law to that extent.

Stewart stood up and walked to the window. 'The first we knew he'd married was after his death when the solicitor sent us notification Sean had made a new will. Sean had stipulated that we were not to be told of his funeral until after the event. I gather that was the final wound he wanted to inflict on my mother. I could never forgive him that.'

Desiree felt terrible. 'But surely I would have over-turned that. I can't imagine any woman denying a mother's right to stand at her son's grave.'

Stewart turned to face her but he remained at the window, distanced by more than space between them. 'It seemed not.'

She couldn't read his thoughts as he came and sat back down beside her. His voice was heavy. 'He could have told you he was an orphan. Or who knows what legalities he'd arranged. Sean could be maliciously brilliant.'

Desiree began to seriously wonder why she would have been involved with such a man as Stewart de-scribed. And bear two children by him?

She shook her head. 'It all feels wrong.' She leant

towards Stewart and tried to communicate her deep unease but he was still lost in the past. 'Why would I be attracted to someone of your brother's character?'

'You're a woman.'

Desiree threw her head up at that. 'I beg your pardon?'

Stewart looked up from the contemplation of his nails and smiled slightly at Desiree's ire. He held up his hand. 'Sorry. No disrespect intended.'

'Really? Have a little grudge against women in general, do you?' She'd never have thought so.

'Of course not.'

Liar, she thought, but didn't voice it. Desiree noted his poker face but was too tired to fight now.

He went on. 'Sean was an accomplished ladies' man and could turn on the charm.'

'Like you?'

He smiled at that. 'Much better than me.'

Charm was obviously something the brothers shared, but Stewart obviously had no intention of admitting it.

'Interesting men, the Kramer men.' She stared at him thoughtfully for a moment then shook her head. 'But I can't imagine not contacting your mother, no matter what he'd arranged. All of that behaviour offends me.'

He looked up, recognising she was genuinely sceptical. 'What are you proposing?'

Desiree covered her face with her hands and then pulled them away. 'Check records, I don't know, blood types, DNA on Sophie.' She glanced around the room, becoming agitated again. 'Check the other casualties from the train that might match.'

'For whom?' Stewart spread his hands. 'Another twenty-six-year-old pregnant woman with a one-year-old child?' He held up his hand to placate her. 'As you wish. I will make more enquiries. But doesn't anything about where you are now feel right?'

She sighed. 'I don't feel awkward with Sophie and she seems to recognise me. But to not remember my own child, if Sophie is my child, is unbelievable. Simone is my baby and my greatest concern at the moment. She feels right.'

She met his caring eyes. 'And your face is familiar. Whether that was from the accident or because you look like my husband, I don't know.'

She chewed her lip at the obvious flaw in her argument. 'But if I'm not Desiree…who is Simone's father and why isn't someone else looking for me?'

She searched in the grey nothingness of her memory. Nothing there and nobody home—just empty cupboards and drawers where memories should have been.

There must be something familiar that would strike a chord in her elusive past. Then she thought of the NICU.

'Today, when you took me to the NICU, I felt as if

I knew it or some place like it. I knew it well. It was as if I'd had previous experience with sick babies.'

Stewart was sceptical. 'Perhaps Sophie was premature, as well?'

Desiree sighed as he prosaically agreed with her own reflections and dashed her hopes of a breakthrough. 'It's a possibility.' Her head began to ache and she closed her eyes to block out the light from the window.

'You're tired,' he said, and stood up to draw the blinds. 'I promise I'll recheck the backgrounds.' He smiled wryly. 'I'm actually waiting for some information about you from a private detective. I contacted him when you wrote to say you were coming from Brisbane.'

She winced and hoped they would find nothing unsavoury in her past to change the warm way that Stewart looked at her and then rebuked herself for fanciful notions.

'Go to sleep, Desiree. I'll come back tomorrow. No matter what we find, we'll be here for you and your girls.'

She closed her eyes and felt a light kiss on her forehead before he walked away.

How alone would she feel if Stewart really wasn't her brother-in-law?

Stewart paced his office, unable to work as he waited for the private detective to return his call.

He'd contacted his friend in the police force for a list of the casualties and had been told most, but not all, passengers had been positively identified by friends or relatives.

What if she wasn't Desiree? He couldn't believe he was even thinking that.

He needed the coroner to confirm or deny if there had been another pregnant woman but the idea seemed far-fetched when everything else pointed to Desiree being his sister-in-law.

His police friend would see what he could do.

The problem, of course, was his attraction to Desiree. He was drawn relentlessly, overwhelmingly and despite all his defences to his brother's widow, and that irony would be the greatest laugh his brother would have on him.

He had never thought to want a woman Sean had been with.

These were the last of the personal wounds Sean had inflicted.

Every girl Stewart had favoured in his teens had been systematically seduced by Sean at the first sign of partiality to Stewart.

Too young to shrug off the wounds initially, Stewart had withdrawn from the mating game, more to thwart his brother than to protect himself, yet still some of his betrayal by women remained to isolate him from relationships.

During college he'd met Maria and they had established a long and comfortable relationship but it had taken him years to get around to proposing.

His mother had been thrilled at the prospect of grandchildren, which had influenced him to put his ridiculous insecurities behind him and settle down.

Maria had run away with Sean a month before their wedding. Right after the engagement party! Not quite the invitation he had issued to his brother, he thought bitterly.

Devastated by Maria's fickleness, Stewart had believed his fiancée would be the one woman who would prefer him to Sean. He'd been bitterly disappointed that his brother had felt the need to cause such distress.

He'd thought that because they had been older things would have changed—but, no, Sean had still taken her from him!

Maria's affair with Sean hadn't lasted even to the cancelled wedding date, but Stewart didn't doubt Sean had been imminently satisfied with the damage he'd caused.

Stewart had severed all ties, both social and financial, with the latter hurting Sean the most and the former his mother.

Stewart had sworn off women and withdrawn from the social scene he had never really enjoyed and concentrated on work, and later, when his mother became more ill, he'd savoured what time he had left with the one woman he knew he could trust.

This blazing attraction Stewart fought for Sean's widow must have his brother rolling with glee in his grave.

As for Desiree's professed inability to accept her identity, he didn't know what to make of it. Whether her amnesia was compounded by a disastrous marriage to his brother that she refused to remember, he couldn't tell.

He suspected as much and pitied his niece that her mother had blocked her out as well. Though, to give Desiree her due, she did try to make that up to Sophie.

He'd discussed Desiree's case with her doctor and had been told there was little he could do until her memory started functioning again.

Everything pointed to the fact that she was Sean's wife.

There was very little chance it could be otherwise and, truth be told, he didn't want to think about how he would react if Desiree was not his sister-in-law.

Just because Sean was no longer alive, it didn't mean he himself was any better at holding a woman, or was willing to risk his heart again.

Stewart glared at the phone and as if in capitulation it finally rang. The private detective had no further information on Desiree.

Desiree's doctor looked like a walrus but at least he was pleasant. 'Good morning, my dear, good morning.'

Desiree contemplated another day with no mem-

ories and the need to lean on people she didn't know.
Good, was it? 'Good morning,' she said.

'The best news is all your blood tests returned
even better than I had expected. If you feel well
enough to go home, you would be able to leave this
afternoon after the last blood results come through.'

Desiree smiled noncommittally. Home? Where
was her home? 'Thank you.'

'You must be accompanied, of course, and stay
with supervision for the next few days, but I understand Stewart Kramer is taking care of that for you.'

It wasn't her doctor's problem, she thought, so
didn't dispute his happy ending. 'That's right.' She
sighed and wished it would all get easier. 'What about
my memory?'

Dr Walrus twirled his moustache. Now she
couldn't even remember his correct name. The doctor
went on. 'You did have a nasty blow to your head.
There will still be swelling and perhaps the bruised
area of your brain will take a while to recover. There
is no way of knowing when or even if your memory
will return.'

'I see.' Such a cheerful guy but she'd expected that
answer.

Dr Walrus must have picked up on her thoughts
because he lifted a finger and shook it. 'Be thankful
timely blood transfusions have prevented long-term
damage to your organs.' He stepped forward and tilted
her face to examine her cheek and the sutures on her

wrist. 'All healing well,' he pronounced. 'Sutures out in five days.'

He looked at her under his bushy brows and winked. 'Your Sophie is full of life and also doing very well, apart from minor kidney bruising. Perhaps tomorrow she will be able to go home, too.'

'We were both very fortunate.' Except for who I am, where I came from and the last twenty-five to thirty years of my life that I seem to have misplaced, she thought, but she was fortunate.

'Stewart says your wee baby is a fighter as well.'

'Simone is stable, thank you.' Thank God, she thought, and doubted she would cope if Simone's condition deteriorated. 'She will be a patient here for a while yet, though.'

The good news about Sophie's improved condition brightened Desiree's morning but couldn't lift the guilt she carried.

It sat uncomfortably that she felt so much closer to Simone, and her premature baby's health, than Sophie in the children's ward. What sort of mother was she? Maybe she did suit the monster she had married as painted by Stewart?

Leanore arrived to visit mid-morning and Desiree greeted her arrival as a welcome distraction from such depressing thoughts. The wheelchair was pushed by a tall, stout woman with a ready smile. There was no sign of Stewart.

Desiree smiled at her mother-in-law and pushed

away the disappointment that she had no right to feel, just because Leanore wasn't followed in by her younger son. 'It's good of you to come, Mrs Kramer.'

'You are welcome, my dear.' Leanore kissed her cheek and then sat back down in her chair to introduce her companion. 'This is Winny. My housekeeper and my keeper, so I don't get lost.'

'Nice to meet you, Winny.' She shook hands with the stout woman and kindness seemed to flow from her warm fingers to Desiree.

Winny pumped her hand. 'I'm pleased to meet you, Mrs Kramer.'

Desiree blinked at the title and name. She couldn't see herself ever getting used to being called Mrs Kramer.

Winny unwrapped a bunch of roses and Desiree looked across at Leanore's bright, enquiring eyes.

What did you talk about with a mother-in-law when you couldn't remember the one person she wanted to hear about? Desiree studied the older lady as Leanore discussed the flowers with Winny.

What she saw diffused any awkwardness she'd felt. Yesterday she hadn't noticed the faint yellow tinge to Leanore's skin or the greyness around her mouth. Even the lack of balance in her chair was noticeable, let alone when she stood. Stewart's mother was far from well and that would explain her forgetfulness, too.

There was a crack in the clouds of her memories

and a shaft of knowledge of the disease process broke through.

Desiree clutched the bedclothes in excitement. Was it coming back? Did she remember that Leanore had such an illness? She remembered helping someone into a wheelchair before.

No. She hadn't met Leanore previously. Then the feeling was gone and she was left with no further clue. Desiree bit her lip in disappointment and tried to pay attention to Leanore's conversation. It was so unfair she couldn't remember.

'Stewart flew to Brisbane for something or other but he'll be home this evening.' Leanore looked across at Winny for confirmation. 'It was this evening, wasn't it, Winny?'

Winny nodded. 'The sister said you can be discharged this afternoon, Mrs Kramer, and Sophie tomorrow. We're all so excited.'

Desiree doubted 'excited' was the word Stewart was thinking, if he knew, but she let that pass. There was definitely a tiny dusting of pink in Leanore's sallow cheeks and a sparkle in the faded blue eyes at the thought of their arrival, so that was a good thing.

Leanore planned ahead as she directed Winny how to arrange the fresh flowers on the shelf. 'Would you like to wait for Stewart to pick you up or shall I send the driver?'

Desiree hadn't thought that far and it was daunting. 'If you don't mind, I'll wait for Stewart. Perhaps he could help with the discharge paperwork I'd be a little vague with.'

Vague was an understatement. Desiree's brain was an empty filing cabinet and the sliding drawers echoed every time she tried to pin her past to a folder.

Finished with supervising Winny's efforts, Leanore leaned towards the bed. 'How is the littlest girl today?'

'Simone,' Winny reminded Leanore gently.

Leanore lowered her voice as if she were afraid of anyone hearing. 'It's a bit silly when my son is in charge there, but I don't like to go down to that place without Stewart. Actually, I don't like it at all. All those machines and sick babies upset me.'

Desiree smiled as Leanore crinkled her nose. 'Simone is doing as well as we can hope. She doesn't seem to have any serious problems at the moment, thank goodness, and we can just pray that she continues to grow without setbacks.'

Leanore squeezed her fingers together in relief. 'I'm pleased you're all going to stay with us. It was such a lift when we heard you were coming. I'd been so depressed since Sean's death that nothing seemed to matter any more. I know Stewart was at his wits' end with me. Poor boy.'

Desiree suppressed a smile at the thought of the eminent consultant labelled a boy.

Leanore paused and then sat forward on her chair. Her voice lowered conspiratorially. 'Stewart told me not to pester you with questions about Sean, but it is hard. I missed the last years of his life and I'd love to hear…'

Her voice trailed off and she opened her bag and took out a lacy handkerchief to wipe her eyes. 'I'm a foolish woman because Sean wasn't a model son at all, but he was my firstborn, and I could forgive him anything.'

'I'm sorry I can't remember anything to give you comfort,' Desiree said gently. 'If I do think of anything about him, you will be the first to know.'

Leanore sniffed and sat straighter. 'You're a good girl, I could tell from the first moment. Stewart didn't need to be worried at all.'

She looked across at Winny. 'We've opened up the nursery again, haven't we?'

Leanore's eyes filled again and she didn't wait for the answer from her housekeeper. 'It was strange to see the toys my boys had played with, or should I say fought over.' She chuckled. 'They were such boys. Always fighting. Sean couldn't bear to see Stewart with a toy that he fancied.'

'Does it hurt you to talk about Sean and Stewart when they were younger? I'd like to know more and maybe it will even bring back some memories of my own.'

It seemed that Leanore would like nothing more. 'I remember the past so much better than the present, so that's easy. The boys were devils.' She smiled gently at the memories. 'Although Stewart became more responsible the wilder Sean became.'

Desiree guessed that was how it had continued as she settled down to listen to her new mother-in-law.

Oddly, the anecdotes about Stewart she found more interesting than those of her supposed dead husband.

'I can't wait to have children in the house again, and neither can Winny.'

Desiree reached over and touched the wrinkled hand that rested on the bedside. 'I don't know how long I will stay but we will visit you often.'

Leanore turned her face away. 'Let's not talk about you going when you haven't even arrived yet.'

Desiree left that battle for another time.

Late that afternoon, Stewart searched out Desiree in the NICU. He'd tried the children's ward but she'd already left after Sophie's tea and bottle and had moved on to visit Simone.

He imagined motherhood could be surprisingly exhausting, especially after a major shock such as Desiree had suffered. He needed to ensure she didn't do too much.

His step quickened unconsciously as he left the sink inside the NICU door and walked the length of the room.

He could see Simone had fallen to Gina's case load again, which was good. Desiree and Gina seemed to get on well. Patient allocation was planned that way to give the babies and the parents some continuity of care.

Gina had already spoken to him about how Desiree could be competently involved in Simone's care and it seemed she had been right. Desiree looked extremely competent.

Stewart's eyebrows rose as he watched the two of them. Desiree knew exactly what she was doing.

There was no hesitation about the way Desiree lifted Simone, with all her tubes attached, while Gina made the bed underneath the baby's tiny nappied bottom.

The oxygen saturation alarm was activated by the movements as they resettled Simone and Desiree absently pressed the 'silence' button with one hand while she adjusted Simone's head position.

She was so confident. Her movements around the crib all precisely organised and focussed.

It made sense. After what he'd found out today. This woman was no actress. No fashion plate living the high life with his brother.

He tried to imagine the impact of being told that you were a widow, had another child, that you were someone else from whom you felt inside.

He'd done that to her, even though unintentionally, and he hoped she would forgive him. He wondered, maybe even hoped, that she'd be as glad that she hadn't been married to his brother as he was.

'Hello, there,' he said as he closed the gap between them. She looked more beautiful than he remembered and he resisted the sudden urge to kiss her cheek. He'd never been a cheek kisser but that sudden surge of joy at seeing her finally made him understand how the practice had come about.

Desiree turned her face slowly away from the crib, as if checking she'd left all correct, before transferring her attention.

'Hello, Stewart. How was Brisbane?' She switched the 'silence' on the pulse oximeter back to 'enable' now that they had finished the bed change. Second nature, he could see that now. And she was calm. Her aura was calm and he felt the pull of attraction again.

Gina looked from one to the other and stepped away to the sink to wash her hands before checking on her other charge.

He shrugged his shoulders to lose some of the tension he's felt on the way here. He had to do this right. 'Brisbane was hot. You seem to know your way around the crib.' She smiled at his observation and he thought how easy it was to watch her.

She looked earnestly up into his face. 'I told you I felt at ease here. If Sophie wasn't prem, I believe Desiree must have been a nurse.'

'Desiree Kramer was an actress and she died tragically in a train crash. However, you, Amanda Edwards, a neonatal nurse from Brisbane, survived.'

CHAPTER FIVE

AMANDA'S world tilted again and the room faded with the impact of her name. A wave of heat hit her and then a shower of cold and she swayed.

Stewart's arms came around her and she sagged against him. Her voice seemed to come from along way off. 'I'm not Desiree?'

When the blackness receded it was the disappointment that surprised Amanda most. How ridiculous to be upset she wasn't Desiree.

Stewart pulled the stool over and Amanda slid onto it with shaky legs.

His face looked as pale as hers felt. 'That was very badly done. I'm sorry, Amanda. The words tumbled out in the worst possible way and I wish I could call them back. Damn. This was not how I planned it.'

She barely heard Stewart's words, though she could see he was distressed. At least her instincts hadn't been mistaken. She hadn't been married to a man she was sure she would have despised—or had been such an atrocious mother she'd forgotten her own one-year-old child.

It was relief that made her feel weak. She hadn't committed either sin but she would miss Sophie. Her stomach plummeted. She'd miss all of her new family.

Stewart ran his fingers through his hair and crouched down to see her face, and with his brow creased in concern he appeared more upset than she was. Obviously he hadn't known how she would take it.

She didn't know how she felt herself yet. Amanda shook her head and waved him on.

He sighed. 'You wouldn't believe me if I told you I spent the flight from Brisbane trying to work out the gentlest way to tell you and then blew it all like that.'

'Stop worrying. At least Amanda as a name sounds more me than Desiree,' she said through teeth that suddenly chattered. He took her hands in sympathy and rubbed them.

'I'll get you some water.'

Amanda watched him hurry away and she closed her eyes and shuddered at the thought of how she would have to piece together a past from nothing—again.

She was as adrift at this moment as when she'd woken up two days ago—the thought was terrifying because this time there would be no Stewart to protect her from harsh realities.

For someone she had known for such a short time his impact had been enormous.

She hadn't been thrilled with being Desiree but at least that name had come with a family—a family that had welcomed her in a way that it would be hard to lose now.

Cold reality seeped in with no comfort. Amanda Edwards obviously had not been missed by anyone.

No person cared that she hadn't arrived safely in Sydney, had been injured and nearly killed, or that her premature daughter was fighting for her life.

Who was her daughter's father? Was he searching for them? Was there someone she had to tell about Simone's birth?

Stewart came back with the water. 'Drink this.'

Amanda opened her eyes and took the paper cup. The water slid down her throat and cooled some of the agitation she was feeling but didn't bridge the chasm that had just opened in front of her.

She needed information. 'Tell me everything. How did you find out who I was?'

'I discovered your identity through the casualty list from the train. You asked me to check and you were right. There was another woman your age, she was pregnant, and she matched photographs that were faxed from the private detective this morning. Sophie is her daughter and the dead woman was my sister-in-law, Desiree Kramer.'

She really wasn't Desiree. 'There's more, isn't there?' It was better that she heard it all because she needed to build her life all over again and somewhere to start would help. Right at this moment she didn't even know if she could find the energy to try.

She felt like screaming about the unfairness of losing her identity twice, even though she would much rather not have been Desiree.

'Desiree's original identification had been yours.'

He paused and Amanda steeled herself.

'Amanda Edwards's body was identified by a distressed nurse from a Brisbane hospital who had been on the train. She'd stumbled across Desiree's body in the confusion and identified her as you. I flew up there this morning to see that nurse at home. She was shocked and very glad she'd made a mistake and apologised profusely. She sends her love and wishes for a speedy recovery.'

'At least I had one friend.' She wondered if her one friend was the only person in the world who cared fleetingly whether she lived or died.

'There's not much more to tell but I think that's enough for now. You've had a shock and I'm kicking myself I started this here.'

He looked around for Gina. 'Let me take you home. Everything is prepared for your arrival. Obviously you can come back here to see Simone whenever you want, but I think you should rest now.'

The implications of this discovery for Amanda sank in further and she looked up at him. 'You don't have to take me to your home now.'

His face softened, as did his voice. 'That hasn't

changed.' At that moment Amanda didn't have the strength to fight the relief that washed over her.

Stewart looked around and the intensity of his gaze made Gina scurry over instantly.

Amanda's pale face had him kicking himself for his handling of this. She had done remarkably well to stay composed, and conscious by the look of her face, and he had to get her home before she fell down.

'I'd like to take you home now.' Stewart kept his arm under hers, afraid her legs would give way.

'Simone's mother is leaving,' Stewart said to Gina. 'She's had a shock but she'll be back in the morning.'

Amanda felt a bubble of hysterical laughter rise like bile in her throat but she bit it back grimly. So 'Simone's mother' was his name for her. She doubted it would be appropriate to laugh at her demotion from sister-in-law to stranger.

'You can contact her on my home number,' Stewart said to Gina over his shoulder as he steered Amanda back towards the door.

Amanda went through the checking-out-from-hospital process in a foggy haze. Stewart discharged her as Desiree Kramer. Amanda was too mentally exhausted to demur.

'I'll sort all that out later,' Stewart promised. 'I need to get you home,' he said, just as a flash bulb exploded in their faces.

The media were waiting at the bottom of the stairs.

This was something she hadn't expected. Amanda found herself tucked under Stewart's arm as he shouldered a way through the throng to the car park.

'How are you feeling now? Did you know you and your baby were the only survivors in the first two carriages, Mrs Kramer? Eye witnesses say you crawled out with the baby down your shirt. Can you describe your ordeal?'

The questions swirled around her, and if she hadn't had Stewart protecting her, Amanda would have fainted from the confusion.

'Hang in there,' Stewart soothed in an undertone. To the press of bodies he was calm. 'Give her a break, guys. Her baby is doing well and she needs a rest.'

He steered her towards the doctors' car park and she heard the beep-beep of the door lock before she saw the car. It was large and black and she finally grasped the advantage of tinted windows. Almost before she knew it he had her seated in the car and had started the engine.

Her pulse hammered in her throat. 'I didn't expect that.'

'You're news. The bystanders saw you crawl from the carriage carrying Sophie. You were the one good story in a situation of horror. It is better that they see you so the story can blow over. I won't let them annoy you.'

He was protecting her again. 'It's not your problem,' Amanda said in a flat voice. 'I'm not your problem.'

'We're at odds there, but we'll talk about it later,' Stewart said as they pulled out of the car park to more camera flashes.

'When I leave your house I will have to manage,' Amanda mumbled.

Stewart eased into traffic and glanced across at her when he'd made the outside lane. 'I'm not going to send you out into the world just because I know you're not Desiree.'

Stewart spoke quietly but with enough conviction to cause Amanda to turn his way.

'I can't accept your help.' Her thoughts slipped out verbally. 'You've gone out of your way to look after me since I woke up and you didn't need to. You wouldn't have if you'd known we weren't related. And we aren't. You have enough problems with an orphaned niece and an ill mother.'

'Yes, my mother is ill but we have many good days ahead of us yet.'

'So you don't need more dependants.'

Stewart obviously didn't see it that way. 'You are no dependant. You saved my niece's life and risked your own in doing so. Our family owes you a huge debt. You can let us look after you at least until you have somewhere else to go.'

It would be so easy to listen to him. To leave the

logistics of finding a place to sleep, a way to keep visiting her daughter until Simone was well enough to be discharged from hospital, a job to fund it all and not worry about the fact that nobody else cared.

But the problems wouldn't go away. She needed to find out who she really was, somewhere to live, some way to support herself and her daughter. She needed to find out who the father of her baby was.

Goodness knew why she had left Brisbane for Sydney at such an inconvenient time when it was all going to be so hard.

Tiredness suddenly overwhelmed her and Amanda could barely keep her eyes open.

'Leave it, Amanda.' Stewart's voice drifted across from the other side of the car. 'There's time to worry when you feel better. Rest back in the seat and I'll wake you when we get home.'

Stewart's home!

The house was two-storied and multi-gabled with a walled fence and beautiful gardens. He opened her car door and Amanda accepted his arm for assistance.

The entry hall, all black and white tiles and soaring ceiling, made Amanda even more aware of the torn coat and borrowed slippers she'd left the hospital in. Stewart's housekeeper came hurriedly from a room down the hall to welcome them.

'Winny, I believe you've met our guest. This is Miss Amanda Edwards, not Mr Sean's wife, as we thought, but a very valued friend of the family. We owe her a huge debt of gratitude for caring for my niece in the recent tragic events.'

The older woman nodded as she tried to understand the ramifications of Stewart's news.

Stewart spoke more slowly. 'My brother's wife did not survive the accident. Sophie, did, thanks to Miss Edwards.'

'Wel-welcome Miss Edwards.' Winny almost curtsied and Amanda didn't know what to do.

'Hello again, Winny. Please, call me Amanda.' This time her name came easily for a change. 'I do hope it's not too much trouble, me coming here.'

Here, it seemed, Winny was on surer ground. 'Oh, no, miss. It's no trouble at all. Some days I'm looking for trouble in this quiet house.'

Stewart raised one eyebrow in amusement and Amanda smiled tiredly. 'I'll try not to be too exciting, Winny.'

'It's Miss Sophie that has the house on its ears,' confided Winny, and Amanda confirmed her first impressions that the housekeeper was a kindly soul.

Sophie would be fine with this woman. 'She's a lovely child and far too young to lose her mother,' Amanda said.

Winny's eyes filled with tears. 'That's true, miss, but now she has a family and all waiting for her.'

Stewart broke in. 'Why don't you show Miss Edwards to her room to freshen up before dinner?

She's very tired. I'll find my mother and explain the new developments.'

'Certainly, sir.'

New developments all right, Amanda thought grimly as she followed Winny up the stairs. New headache, new worries and all on top of the constant fear that Simone would run into one of the myriad problems prematurity could bring.

Stewart watched Amanda climb the stairs, her hand gripped the banister as if to pull her weight up. He could almost feel the weariness in her bowed head.

There was too much to do at this moment to follow the direction his thoughts wanted to take. His hands clenched with the urge to lift Amanda's drooping body into his arms and save her the effort of each step.

But that was ridiculous and he doubted she'd thank him. He barely knew the woman and she occupied too many of his thoughts already no matter how hard he fought to dismiss her from his mind.

All these years he'd laughed at people who professed to have recognised the one person for them and now his heart was hinting at the same. He, who'd sworn off all women, had begun to wonder.

If he wasn't careful Amanda would imprint her face indelibly onto his heart and his life before he knew it. Especially now the hurdle of being his brother's wife had been removed and he could admit to himself how deep his attraction to her really was.

That moment in time from two days ago when she'd lifted her eyes and collapsed into his arms replayed in his mind a dozen times a day.

In the next few complicated weeks he would help her sort out this mess, help her through the trials of caring for her baby, and then they would see. He couldn't deny there was a certain apprehension about the outcome. He wasn't sure he was ready to trust again or had the courage to welcome Amanda into his life.

But for now there was much to do. He needed to arrange the real Desiree's funeral, find any relatives she had left, sort out his brother's wife's affairs and ensure his niece was safely in his own custody. Then he would re-evaluate his intentions towards Miss Amanda Edwards.

CHAPTER SIX

WINNY showed Amanda into a spacious room complete with bay window overlooking the trees in the garden below. Her headache throbbed in time to her heartbeat as she assured Winny she would be very comfortable.

The memories gathered like thunder on the horizon, and by the time Winny left she could barely see for the cloud that hovered in her mind.

She needed to remember the missing pieces of her previous life but the feeling came with a pounding headache that sapped her energy.

Apprehension lifted the hairs on the back of her neck and it was when Amanda sank back on the bed and glanced across the room straight into the oval mirror that suddenly the room began to swirl around and she was swept into the past. The memories flooded through her mind with all the distress she had feared in regard to the accident.

* * *

For Amanda Edwards on the train from Brisbane, it had all started with a conversation. The midday sun shone through the windows of the carriage as they sped past the calming waters of the Hawkesbury River towards Sydney. Across from Amanda a baby fussed.

'Your daughter is beautiful.' Amanda smiled at the fashionably dressed woman in the seat opposite her.

'Yes. She's usually a good girl for the nanny. But now she doesn't want her bottle from me.' The mother's slim fingers shook with stress. 'Do you think you could you hold her while I get her pram ready?'

Without hesitation Amanda took the infant and the mother sighed with relief when the baby stopped crying.

The little girl looked hungry to Amanda's practised eye. 'Can I try the bottle?'

The woman shrugged and handed the formula to Amanda who teased the little one's lips with the teat until the baby decided she was thirsty.

'Typical.' The baby's mother shook her head.

Amanda smiled. 'Sometimes babies are fickle, especially when they are travelling and everyone is tired. What's your daughter's name?'

The woman brushed a strand of wayward hair out of her eyes. 'Sophie, and I'm Desiree.' Under the heavy make-up she looked strained.

Desiree frowned, a little put out at the settled infant in Amanda's competent arms. 'You must have children of your own.'

Amanda smiled. 'Not yet.' She patted her rounded stomach. 'Soon! I'm not due for almost three months. I'm a paediatric and neonatal nurse so I've had lots of practice with other people's babies, but not my own.'

Amanda swallowed the lump that came to her throat with those words. Her life was in a messy puddle around her feet but at least she'd shaken off the mud that Craig had slung at her. The lies he'd told about her shouldn't have hurt as much as they had.

St Meredith's in Sydney had offered to take her until near the end of her pregnancy because she hadn't wanted to go back to her training hospital and parade the results of her naïve foolishness over a certain consultant.

She had her late aunt's house to go to. The tenants had moved out yesterday and with work she could manage until her baby was born. It would be good for her self-esteem to have her own place and learn to be self-sufficient again. Hopefully she would be set up enough until she could return to work.

At least she could look up old friends when she stopped feeling like a fool. She'd only followed Craig to Brisbane two years ago.

Absently Amanda gently patted Sophie's back. She had to believe things would improve.

'I'm an actress.' Desiree smiled wanly and Amanda focussed on the mother of the child she was holding.

'At least I was before Sophie happened,' Desiree said. 'Now I'm a widow with my next baby due around May, too. I don't know how I'll manage.'

She glanced at her watch. 'Hopefully my husband's relatives like children. I find it difficult enough with one baby even though I had Nanny up until yesterday.'

Desiree pulled the pram towards her and lifted the fluffy blankets. Sophie burped indelicately on Amanda's shoulder and both women smiled as Amanda handed the little girl back and watched her mother strap her in.

'Nanny said she sleeps well even in her pram after her feed,' Desiree said.

'Would you like me to rinse the bottle out for you at the water dispenser?' Amanda offered.

'I'll go. I need to dash and put my lippy on before we arrive. Sophie seems to keep me untidy.' Desiree frowned and gestured at her hair and a comb and lipstick she'd taken from the bag. 'Will you mind my baby and my bag?'

Amanda wondered what had happened to 'Nanny' as she looked at the bulky soft leather backpack. 'No problem. Better be quick. I think we're slowing down.'

The backpack, the pram, the baby and mother's clothes all shrieked money and Amanda wondered briefly why this woman was travelling by train and not in a hire car.

She waved Desiree off and they both patted discernible stomachs, two dark-haired young women in the prime of their lives. Desiree moved quickly towards the rest rooms in the first carriage.

At that moment, as she opened the door between the carriages, the air seemed to shimmer with a blast of pressure and the screech of metal on metal and the crash of two solid objects colliding at great speed.

In a frozen fraction of a second, luggage and people flew from one end of the carriage to the other as the air was filled with screams from the passengers. The last thing Amanda saw was the body of the baby's mother hurtling away from her through the door into the next carriage.

It was all there for Amanda to remember.

That poor young woman.

Poor Desiree. How unbelievable that she, Sophie and Simone had survived, and beautiful Desiree had perished.

The time between the accident and waking up in hospital was still patchy. She accepted sadly she would probably never remember Simone's birth but that was a small price to pay for Simone's survival.

Amanda tried to imagine how different the last couple of days would have been if Stewart hadn't assumed she was Desiree.

How different it would have been to wake up with no support, no one to help her come to grips with

Simone's birth and no one to make her welcome in their home until she found her feet.

Now that her memory had shifted, uneven chunks of her life were there to call on. Her early life she could see in full Technicolor.

Her childhood, brought up by her dear Aunt Millie after her parents died. Her teens, taking over the role of carer for her aunt during the years it had taken for cancer to claim Millie.

Amanda had seen through the roller-coaster of rapidly growing brain tumours during Millie's last year of life and the good times had been like gold and something she would never regret.

After her aunt's death Amanda had attended university, thanks to Millie's bequest, and had found her niche in neonatal and children's nursing.

She remembered falling in love with Craig. He'd seemed like a God. Imagine, the consultant of the NICU asking her out.

He'd pursued her, asked her to marry him, and then whisked her to Brisbane when he'd taken over the consultancy at Mothers and Babies.

She'd been thrilled as she'd set up his beautiful house over the Brisbane River, planned their wedding, and worked part time in the unit in the job he'd secured for her.

Life had been wonderful but they hadn't discussed a family.

She'd suggested they take extra precautions after

her stomach bug but he'd airily waved her concerns away. That was why it had been such a shock when he'd been horrified about her pregnancy.

The paediatrician in charge of Brisbane Babies had suddenly had grander plans for his dynasty than Amanda Edwards's child.

She remembered his inexplicable campaign to discredit her at work—until she'd realised he'd fallen for the CEO's daughter.

Their relationship had disintegrated fairly quickly after that.

What a disaster her first love had been. She supposed she should at least tell him of their daughter's birth but she doubted he'd care.

All she'd thought of when packing had been the safety and comfort of Aunt Millie's house. Thank goodness she hadn't sold it when Craig had suggested she do so.

Now, with the return of her memory, moving interstate in the last trimester of her pregnancy to Sydney made perfect sense. She'd come home.

Someone knocked on the door of her room and a few seconds later Winny opened the door with one hand. She balanced a teatray with the other.

The big woman's comforting presence did a lot to slow Amanda's racing heartbeat and she took a few calming breaths as more of her past slid into place.

Amanda hurried to her feet to help the older

woman but her head swam as she stood up and she swayed unsteadily.

'Sit down, miss. You're as pale as a ghost.' Winny placed the tray on the bedside table and hurried to rest her hand on Amanda's shoulder to keep her in her seat.

She was nobody to this woman and yet she cared. Amanda felt tears sting behind her eyes at Winny's concern.

'I feel like I've seen more than a ghost. Some of my memory has come back in a bit of a rush, Winny. But I'm feeling better now.'

Amanda's dizziness receded as the seconds passed and she sniffed the threatening tears away. She'd been alone before Craig and had managed perfectly well.

'Shall I ask the doctor to come up, miss? I'm not sure you look a hundred per cent.'

'I'll be fine.' No doubt she was still shocked and that was why she wanted to burst into tears at the slightest kindness. 'Your tea will do the trick.' She took a sip to prove it. 'Wonderful.'

Winny didn't look convinced. 'If you're sure... Dr Stewart will see you in the library in an hour. Will that be all right?'

'Fine. Thank you.' She looked at the kindness in Winny's eyes and promised herself she wouldn't take advantage of these lovely people for too long. 'I see there is a telephone in here. Would it be all right if I used it to ring the hospital about my daughter?'

'That phone was installed yesterday for your arrival, miss. Dr Stewart was very particular it should be here for you so you must use it.'

'He's been very thorough and thoughtful.'

'He is a true gentleman…' Winnie paused and then rushed on. 'He would make any young woman a fine husband and with Miss Sophie needing a mother and all…' Winny didn't wink but she may as well have.

Amanda didn't know where to look. The faithful woman's championship of Stewart wasn't necessary. Amanda didn't doubt Stewart would be a good husband, just that a relationship with a man was the last thing she needed at the moment.

Winny went on. 'Yes, he's a true gentleman, not like his brother, though I shouldn't speak ill of the dead. If you'll excuse me, miss.' Winny pursed her lips and withdrew, as if glad to have said her piece.

'Lucky I didn't marry Sean, then,' Amanda murmured to herself as Winny shut the door. It was obvious Winny thought it high time Stewart wed but Amanda had no plans other than seeing her daughter well and out of hospital.

Until that time she didn't care if Mr Universe needed a wife.

Amanda glanced at the phone. She'd ring the hospital to check on Simone.

Amanda was put on hold and then put through to Gina, who said Simone was asleep and wonderfully stable, and gave a brief run-through of her latest pathology results. All stats were normal and Amanda sighed with relief. She assured Gina she felt better, and hung up.

Her other worries were minor. As soon as Simone was strong enough they would start a new life and she would manage perfectly well as a single mother.

Amanda glanced at the phone again and decided against notifying Craig about Simone.

The thought of speaking to him held no attraction and he'd requested she didn't contact him. She decided she would fax him a summary of Simone's condition with the hospital's address. After what he'd done to her, she owed him nothing more.

An hour later Amanda had finally navigated herself to the library on the ground floor and had seen more of the house than she'd intended.

She'd taken a short cut down the back stairs and ended behind the kitchen, past a breakfast room and into a conservatory. When she'd retraced her steps she'd ended back on her own floor, past half a dozen unoccupied rooms and a sitting room until she'd found the main stairs.

Finally at the library door she hesitated before entering but as soon as Stewart caught sight of her he rose and crossed the room swiftly to her. She could almost believe he was glad to see her.

'So you've rested?' he asked.

Amanda nodded. 'I'm fine.' She went further into the room and admired the original Arthur Streeton painting above the fireplace. She'd seen one with a similar theme in a museum. These people were way out of her league.

Stewart studied her. 'You're pale. Winny said you felt dizzy and had remembered some details.'

Too many unpleasant ones, she thought, but all she said was, 'I have.'

He frowned. 'Sit down. We can wait until you are comfortable before we talk about it.'

He drew her over towards a formal seating arrangement in front of the tall windows and she perched on the edge of one of the overstuffed chairs while he fussed to see she was settled.

'This is a good sign. If some of your memory has come back, it is more likely the rest will come. Be patient.'

'I know.' She grimaced. 'I'm trying to be.'

'I think you're doing amazingly well.' Stewart smiled and Amanda began to feel warm again for the first time since the memories had chilled her more than an hour ago. How could he do that just by looking at her?

'So tell me. How did your memories unfold? When did it happen?' She doubted he was really as interested as he looked but she had to admire his manners.

What had she been doing? Then she remembered. 'The memories shifted when I saw the mirror upstairs.'

'That easy, eh?' He raised one ironic eyebrow and she smiled at his facial acrobatics.

His comment was perceptive. 'It wasn't pleasant, but suddenly there were fragments of images and memories from the accident. I remember quite a lot actually but there are still holes. I'm not complaining, though. Now at least I can remember my life before the accident.'

'So who is Amanda Edwards?' And because of the gentleness in his voice, the walls she'd erected around her fragile emotions trembled. She clutched at her composure and resisted the urge to throw herself on his chest and soak up the comfort that she somehow knew he would more than competently bestow.

Amanda swallowed the lump in her throat and drew a deep breath, consciously relaxing her shoulders. She hoped she could finish this without him seeing how little she looked forward to the next few weeks.

'For the last two years I've worked in Brisbane Babies in the neonatal unit,' she said. 'So that would be why I felt so at ease in Simone's unit.'

'Of course.' He inclined his head. 'And Simone's father?'

Those memories hadn't been so pleasant. 'Someone who worked there.' That left the story untold but the last couple of days had certainly relegated her ex-fiancé to where he belonged in the scheme of things.

Stewart leaned forward. 'Did this…?' He paused. 'Did this man know about your pregnancy?'

Amanda grimaced. 'I gather it was a motivating factor in ending our relationship.'

'Nice guy.'

Amanda shrugged wryly. 'I used to think so. Now I'm just glad he's not a part of our lives. I'll notify him of Simone's birth but I imagine I won't hear anything back.'

Simone's condition had ousted any pain she felt from Craig's desertion into oblivion. Life and Simone were too precious to waste lamenting an untrustworthy man.

'Not everyone is like that.'

Amanda looked up at Stewart's insight into what she hadn't discussed, but dismissed any significance in his comment. He was guessing.

Stewart went on. 'So what were you going to do? What plans did you have when you decided to come to Sydney?'

'The idea of a fresh start was a motivating factor. I lived in Sydney up until two years ago and my late aunt left me a small terrace house in Darlinghurst. The tenants were moving out the day before I arrived so at least I have somewhere to go.'

There. She'd said it. She'd made the first step towards leaving.

She went on. 'St Meredith's had agreed to take me for eight weeks but I'll have to check with them now that Simone is a patient there. I'd saved up enough to set up house for Simone and myself for maternity leave after that.'

He inclined his head as he considered her plans.

Stewart didn't say anything more for a moment. He suspected there was something else that upset her, most probably graphic memories of the accident, and he supposed she needed more time to trust him. He didn't know why that irked him.

He watched her sigh with relief when he didn't comment more about her motivation and his concern deepened.

He inclined his head. 'You could still stay here for a week or two.'

'I shouldn't be here now.'

'You could still work at St Meredith's if that is where you were contracted.' Stewart thought the idea would not appeal now but apparently he was mistaken.

Amanda chewed her lip. 'I would like to but didn't think they'd be interested if my own daughter was a patient.'

Stewart frowned. 'It shouldn't be a problem if you are sure that's what you want to do.'

Amanda half smiled at his assumption that all she had to do was ask.

Somehow she doubted St Meredith's would tell Stewart she wasn't wanted, but she was pretty sure they'd tell her.

Despite that worry, some of the darkness of the afternoon began to seep away. It felt nice to have a champion for a change. There hadn't been many of those in her life that she could remember.

He went on. 'I'm sure you are professional enough

to be able to carry out your duties. Experienced neonatal nurses are scarce on the ground in Sydney. and I heard a rave review of your work in Brisbane.'

So she did have some friends. Craig had driven most of them away with his demands on her time and then his discrediting campaign. She couldn't imagine why she'd let that happen but it was too late now. All she could do was learn from that experience and not rely too heavily on any one person again.

'I do remember I'd researched available work before I moved here. Which reminds me…' she felt her heart race as myriad tasks began to crowd in her head '…I have luggage and furniture in storage.'

It was almost as if he'd read her mind. 'You could stay here for as long as you like. I could arrange for your luggage to come here and your furniture would be fine for the moment. You can do any repairs to your aunt's house before you move in. I can help with un-important things like that while you concentrate on your daughter.'

It was tempting, and she shouldn't be tempted. 'You have your own worries. Desiree's affairs, Sophie, and as you said earlier your mother is far from well.'

His face softened. 'My mother has been in re-mission with metastatic breast cancer. She has been an inspirational survivor and now she has secon-dary tumours in her brain, which affect her memory and gait.'

He smiled ruefully. 'She hates the fact that she is

losing her memory and I'm hoping Sophie's arrival will put joy back into her life and allow her to really savour her last few months. She has been devastated since my brother's death.'

Amanda thought of the kind old lady and her excitement about Sophie's arrival. 'I'm sorry she's not well. My aunt was the same before she died. I cared for her for a year while she was too unsteady to walk on her own and her memory was very erratic. Sometimes the words that came out were nothing like she'd intended.'

They smiled at each other and Stewart grinned. 'My name has many variations. I sometimes have a problem remembering who I am. Then the next minute Mother will be able to tell me the whole family genealogy.'

Amanda remembered Aunt Millie's conversations. 'It was like that with my aunt. Most of the time I could tell what she meant even though the word used was inappropriate. It must be so frustrating for them.'

Stewart nodded. 'It is a bonus that you understand. There are a lot of good days ahead of us yet. Though perhaps you can see my motives for encouraging you to stay are not wholly altruistic,' he said wryly.

He went on. 'I know that Simone is your first priority, as she should be, but perhaps you could think of staying here as separate part-time employment? For Sophie?'

Amanda frowned and wondered if he was concerned

he'd be able to substitute properly as a father for his niece. Did she owe him that support for all the help he'd given her? Or was he just feeling sorry for her?

Stewart continued, 'You would still be free to do shifts in the unit if you wished but I think your presence here could be invaluable and your bank balance would be even healthier when you decided to move out.'

She frowned at what she considered an exaggeration of her versatility. 'I doubt I'd be that useful.'

'You're a paediatric nurse as well. Childhood concerns that my mother would worry about, you would sail over if she had you to consult. And she won't be as well as she is for much longer. Winny will have a lot on her plate.'

Amanda raised her eyebrows sceptically. 'I seem to recall there is an actual paediatrician in the house to consult about childhood illnesses.' Amanda tilted her chin, daring him to dispute that.

He smiled back. 'I work long hours and Sophie likes you. My mother and Winny like you.' He paused. 'I like you.'

She looked away but felt ridiculously flattered at such a simple compliment. 'If in doubt, try flattery?'

Stewart went on as if he'd said nothing unusual. 'We hope you would feel comfortable enough to stay with us for an extended period.'

She couldn't doubt his sincerity. Was it too much to expect them to house a perfect stranger? She did need to settle herself in Aunt Millie's house but the estate agent had hinted there were some repairs required since the last tenant. She would set up her own establishment soon but perhaps she could wait until Simone was well and Stewart's family had settled. It wasn't as if she would stay in this household for ever.

He sensed her hesitation and pressed home his advantage. 'I'm thinking of Sophie when my mother becomes less well. Winny will be heavily involved in my mother's ongoing care. If I can put plans in place to cover that eventuality, it will be less traumatic for Sophie.'

'And when Simone and I move on?' It had to be said.

'We'll worry about that when it happens.' He seemed pretty sure she would stay. The emotionally exhausted side of her said it would be wonderful to sit back and let Stewart continue in control.

But a newly developed caution made Amanda temper her agreement. She felt so uncertain in her own judgement after Craig and the Brisbane disaster that she hesitated. 'It would be easier for me to stay, not a necessity,' Amanda clarified gently but firmly.

'Of course it is your right to decide.' He nodded, and smiled, and the words made sense when he said them. Why did she feel he meant the opposite?

He inclined his head, all innocence. 'Perhaps you would consider delaying your departure and final decision for the next week or two until Simone is more stable?'

'Thank you. A few days here to organise my aunt's house would be easier for me and I do appreciate your help.' She stood up.

He rose as well. 'That would give me time to find someone to share the care for Sophie when she comes home tomorrow.'

Now Amanda felt ungrateful. 'Of course I'll stay until Sophie settles,' she said impulsively. She just wished she could be sure it hadn't been his intention to make her feel that way.

She studied him and the amused glint in his eye warned her he knew what she had been thinking.

'When you read my mind it is quite annoying, you know,' she said conversationally.

'So I believe,' he said, and this time his smile widened to a full grin. He held out his hand. 'To a week at a time, Amanda?'

'To a week for the moment, Stewart.'

CHAPTER SEVEN

SOPHIE settled into the Kramer household next door to Amanda's room as if she belonged there, which, thanks to Stewart assuming guardianship of Sophie, she did. Nobody could imagine life without Sophie.

Even the first night, when Stewart and Amanda stood together and each kissed her brow and tucked her in, the little girl settled easily. She didn't cry in the night and the following nights were no different.

In that first week, when Sophie woke up in the morning, she brought sunshine into all their lives and Leanore especially found joy in her baby ways.

Somehow the time slid into Amanda's second week of residence with a certain poignancy because she knew her time was limited there. For the moment they all had their routines.

On the following Tuesday morning, Leanore and Winny sat and watched while Amanda bathed and dressed Sophie.

Sophie had taken her first steps since arriving and

each day she improved her balance, much to the delight of her grandmother. Sophie didn't mind that her name changed with her grandmother's memory each day.

'See how she walks.' Leanore could barely contain her glee and Winny had tears on her cheeks from laughing.

Sophie felt her way across the room on tottery feet and the toddler's cherubic smiles made the women watching shake with laughter.

Stewart heard the commotion and, absently knotting his tie, he too came to watch Sophie's antics before he left for work. 'You sound like a bunch of hens cackling in here. It's a shame the only rooster has to go to work.'

Amanda glanced up as he stood in the doorway and Sophie bared her sharp little teeth in delight at her new uncle and clapped her hands.

For Stewart, the sun streamed in the window and backlit the gentle smile on Amanda's face as she held his niece's hand. This was how a family should be. This was how he wanted his family to be. A wave of desire hit him firmly in the stomach, snatching away the words he'd been about to say.

He saw Amanda tilt her head questioningly but for the life of him he couldn't get past the moment and produce even a banal comment.

'She's lovely, isn't she?' Amanda looked away from him, stroked the downy soft cheek and hugged Sophie to her. 'Desiree seemed tense but she mentioned a nanny who usually cared for Sophie,' Amanda said. 'Whoever she was, she must have been wonderful because I don't think I've ever seen such a settled child.'

His chest ached from lack of air and with sudden clarity he remembered to refill his lungs. He drew a sharp breath and the warm air rushed into his lungs. This was ridiculous. 'I'll try to track her down if I can.' He knew Amanda would go soon. He hadn't wanted to think about it but he knew her need for independence was never far from her thoughts. Her comment proved it.

Enough. The woman had him spinning like a top and in a place he didn't have the head space to be. What could have been seemed harder to take this morning for some reason.

He turned to his mother. 'I'm off.' He crossed the room and kissed his mother's cheek. 'I love you, Mother, dear. Have a good day. Bye, Winny.'

Then he stepped across and kissed the top of Sophie's hair. 'Bye, Sophie-girl.' She really was a darling, he thought, and couldn't stop the smile at Amanda over the toddler's head. 'Be good for Amanda.'

Amanda blinked at the picture of this tall, distinguished consultant unabashedly telling his mother he loved her then warmly including his new niece, and not an ounce of awkwardness about either action. She shook her head.

Men like this had been out of her orbit—first in her aunt's spinster household and then with Craig's condescending correctness in dealing with most people, including his tiny patients.

She doubted Craig would have welcomed an orphaned niece as warmly into his home and heart as Stewart had.

Imagine if she'd gone ahead and married in Queensland without knowing what to look for in a real man. Those special caring qualities that shone from Stewart Kramer!

Stewart sent her one long measuring look before he turned away and she felt the vibration of his scrutiny in a nervous jangle that brought heat to her skin.

'Have a good morning, Amanda. I'll run your contract by the unit manager when I get a chance and let you know what she says when you come in to see Simone.'

His words were prosaic and had nothing to with the warmth she'd felt from his previous look. He was an intriguing mix but his presence left her feeling very unsettled and it was a good thing she was leaving soon.

Leanore waved to her son as he left and she turned to Amanda. 'He likes you. I can tell. If he marries you I can have more grandchildren like this one. You should probably hurry.'

Amanda willed her heart not to read anything into the fleeting wishes of an ill mother. Of course

Leanore would look for what joy she could find. Thankfully Stewart had already left.

Winny tut-tutted. 'Now, Mrs Leanore, you shouldn't tease Amanda like that.'

Leanore turned to Winny, perplexed. 'Amanda who? I'm talking to this girl here.'

At the hospital later that morning Amanda smiled and chatted to the nurses as she walked the length of the unit to Simone. It was good to be there and distancing herself from the Kramer household. Stewart's house was becoming more like home and less like a stopgap.

She'd do better to feel at home in the NICU and luckily she could see herself working there. That would be one step closer to making a home before Simone's discharge. Today it seemed more urgent that she get on with her life.

Stewart appeared beside her as if conjured up by her arrival. He looked more serious than when he'd left that morning and a tiny flicker of unease pierced her bubble of harmony with the world.

As a neonatal nurse, Amanda had often imagined that if she had a prem baby she would be able to cope with the stress better than an unprepared parent. Faced with the reality of Simone and her prematurity, she had discovered how arrogantly wrong she had been.

Each day held new terrors, new challenges and the ever-present risk of something the doctors couldn't fix. Even with Stewart as her mentor, which was how she thought of him, she woke up sweating in the night and feared for Simone's progress.

Knowing the absolute worst that could happen made her too aware of tiny changes in Simone's health.

Her gaze switched from Stewart to Simone and it was true her daughter's skin colour appeared a little paler than yesterday.

Amanda checked the digital displays on the monitors and, apart from Simone's baseline heart rate, which seemed a little higher, everything appeared normal.

Something was wrong, though. She knew it. Her fingers curled into her palms and she formed the question slowly. 'How is Simone?'

She scrutinised his face and decided his expression was kind. Why? Stewart looked at Simone as well before he answered her. Dread deepened and he must have seen her distress because he moved closer and put his arm around her shoulder to draw him next to her. They faced the crib together.

'Simone is behaving like a typical prem infant. You know the two to three week mark is a time for moments of unusual interest.' His voice was warm and caring, like the arm around her suddenly cold shoulders.

Amanda did know. She steeled herself for bad news. 'Why? What's she doing?'

'She's having a moment of unusual interest. But it will settle.' He gave her shoulders a squeeze and

Amanda relaxed a little against him. He wouldn't be so calm if he was too worried. That was the first thing you learnt when dealing with sick children. Never tempt fate.

'We need to treat her PDA now that she is showing symptoms.'

Patent ductus arteriosis, a failure of the duct between the heart and the lungs to close, was common with premature infants. She knew that a quarter of all preterm infants developed problems and needed treatment.

Sometimes the temporary cardiac plumbing in a baby living via the placenta didn't close and change at birth as it should, but Amanda decided the significance was hugely different when it was your own child.

Stewart pointed out the symptoms they'd noted. 'Her heart rate is up and so is the frequency of her bradycardias and apnoeas.'

The slowing of a baby's heart rate often coincided with periods of the baby not breathing and the frequency of Simone doing that was increasing because of the fault in her blood supply to the heart.

Stewart explained what they'd done. 'We've had to increase her oxygen. The results of the cardiac echo show her heart has a clinically significant patent ductus arteriosus.'

Amanda felt helpless. 'Are you sure she won't need surgery?' Sometimes a surgical tie was required to stop the incorrect blood flow but the operation could have complications and Amanda prayed it wouldn't be necessary.

'I believe not.' His simple confidence allowed Amanda's fear to settle cautiously.

'We've begun treatment with a course of indomethacin for three days. In preterm infants with PDAs, most ducts spontaneously close by the baby's due date or with a month of that date. You know we have good results with that medication at closing the patent ductus and very few side effects.'

'I know.' She sighed. 'It's just harder to hear when your own child is the patient.' She searched his face. If there was more, she wasn't sure she could take it. 'What else?'

'Simone will also need that small amount of packed cell blood transfusion I mentioned the first day. Her red blood cell count has fallen again today. She does have anaemia of prematurity and some jaundice. Are you still happy for her to have that?'

Stewart squeezed her shoulders again and she sighed into him. She nodded. 'Pink and sweet sounds good to me.'

'When all has settled, we'll increase her feeds.' He smiled. 'Every day is a big day when you're as little as Simone is.'

Amanda could see again how he loved his job and cared for every tiny patient he was responsible for. The way he cared for Simone made it easier for her to sleep at night.

It was how paediatricians should be and she was finding it harder to separate the man from the doctor and decide which of his personas she admired most. But that didn't mean she would stay in his house for ever. When Simone left hospital she would leave the Kramer household for good.

'I think you do a great job, Stewart. What I've seen of the unit and the staff…' she looked across at Gina at the next crib '…is totally reassuring, and that usually starts from the top. I'm happy for you to do what's necessary to help Simone adjust.'

'I know that.' He smiled at her. 'Speaking of the staff in the unit, the girls are still doing too many double shifts and would love another experienced neonatal nurse to call on.' He raised his eyebrows. 'What do you think?'

Amanda felt the excitement. She would love that.

He went on. 'Nursing admin are happy for you to start your contract in a couple of weeks, as long as you're not primary carer for Simone, and if you feel able to cope with the workload.'

He looked across the unit to where the NUM chatted with two parents. 'They are prepared to be very flexible. You just need to talk to Claire. As nursing unit manager, she'll slot you in when you're available.'

She could be here more for Simone, even though she wouldn't be caring for her. 'All that with just a mention from you?' Amanda raised her eyebrows.

He shrugged. 'I may have suggested fairly strongly

you would be an asset, but it is up to you to prove it to them.'

Amanda hugged his faith in her to herself.

Was it too early after the accident and Simone's birth to think of working? Simone was getting stronger every day, and apart from this morning had had fewer setbacks than Amanda had anticipated.

Life was settling, things weren't so bad, and she felt appreciated in Stewart's house as well.

Leanore and Winny were dears and Amanda had become used to answering to any name Leanore called her, depending on how clear her mind was that day.

Caring for Sophie was no hardship. The little girl had a sweet nature and had become a part of the household with the minimum of fuss. She bestowed cuddles and giggles on everyone and the house seemed to sing when she was awake. It would be hard to leave.

Amanda knew she needed to start cementing her independence as soon as possible, though. She couldn't coast along here and rely on Stewart's generosity for ever because if she didn't leave soon she might be tempted to dream of permanency, and she needed to prove to herself she could stand alone.

She lifted her chin and made the decision. 'I'll see Claire before I leave today.'

He frowned. 'There's no hurry. Wait until you are ready. We can discuss it tonight before dinner, if you like.'

That feeling of uncertainty left by Craig's betrayal sat coldly in her chest and pushed away the warmth she felt from Stewart. What did Stewart want from her? Was there a motive behind his apparent ease with the present living arrangements? Could she trust his word? Was she just a handy stand-in for Sophie's mother?

There were reasons she shouldn't stay too long with Stewart and his family, not the least being that she needed time to herself to recover from the humiliation she'd faced in Brisbane. She had trust issues that perhaps Stewart didn't deserve but she wouldn't resolve them while living in his house.

'What's wrong?'

How had he picked up on that? 'Nothing. Just a prickle of the skin for lost memories.' She played down the deep unease that continued to gnaw at her.

He looked about to say something else when Gina signalled from further down the unit. He hesitated, sighed, and then turned to move off. He looked back at her. 'Simone will be fine. I'll see you tonight.'

Amanda watched him go but her mind was elsewhere. She needed to visit her aunt's house and begin preparations for moving in, but she couldn't do that while her mind was full of Simone.

Amanda stayed with Simone for the two hours she usually did but she made time to discuss the idea of employment with the unit manager before she left. At least she had made a first step towards separation.

CHAPTER EIGHT

STEWART was often alone in the library before tea and Amanda hurried so she could catch him before the family came down.

At her knock, he closed the screen of his computer and stood up to greet her. The smile he gave and the skidding tingle along her nerves helped strengthen her resolve.

'I need to talk to you.' The words tumbled quickly because she had to begin the separation process—before it became too hard to walk away. When she stepped into the light, his dark brows drew together and he came forward, took her hand and drew her to a seat.

He sat down opposite her and leaned forward. 'You look pale. What can I do to help?'

She tried to marshal her thoughts—the last thing she needed was to appear incoherent—but all she could think about was how close she was to not wanting to leave here. She needed to make the break and make it now.

He smiled to put her at ease. 'I've been told I'm a good listener.'

Amanda sighed at that. The words hung in the air between them and Stewart sat back in his chair and his fingers slipped from hers. She felt the loss keenly but he didn't seem to notice.

'Take your time.' He smiled at her. He looked so big and strong and safe. So capable of managing everything that she began to wonder if she were mad not to just coast along and let Stewart direct the play and see what happened.

Then she remembered doing just that with Craig. 'I spoke to Claire today about part-time work and I've rung the estate agent about picking up the keys to Aunt Millie's house.' She glanced up at him. 'It is time to move out.'

Stewart sat forward, and then he smiled ruefully and sat back again. She felt tears prick her eyes and she blinked them back.

He pursed his lips as if careful of his wording. 'I admire your courage, especially when you have so much on your plate, as well as your concern for Simone. I would like to help you more but I can see you need to start to recapture your independence. I'm sure you will manage brilliantly but I just don't see the need to hurry.'

She felt comfort from his faith in her. 'Thank you.' He had no idea how much his support meant to her. 'You do understand. I want to be settled when Simone comes home from hospital.'

'That won't be for a few weeks yet.'

She shook her head. 'I'm not comfortable imposing on your family.'

'Necessity can be uncomfortable.' The subtle authority in his voice became more noticeable and she saw a little more of the consultant and the man used to having his own way. Her brain seized on this minor arrogance. See, her inner voice confirmed, he's trying to dominate you already.

Then he changed tack. 'Please, stay for the time being. I can help you with little effort. Write down the address of your flat and I'll have the handyman who works here cast his eye over just to make sure it is habitable for Simone and you before you move in.'

'I would prefer to do my own renovations but advice would be helpful. Thank you.'

He nodded. 'You are not alone in this. Save yourself some energy to concentrate on Simone.'

Amanda allowed herself to relax a little. Stewart seemed to understand her need to leave.

Maybe that was all she needed to do before she could get on with her life. It would be wonderful to feel independent again and maybe she would be able to look at Stewart from a distance and find some clarity in her thoughts.

Stewart's mother arrived to join them and nothing further was mentioned about Amanda's impending move.

Stewart stood. 'Would you like a sherry, Mother?'

'Yes, thank you, darling.' Leanore glanced at Amanda and frowned. 'Are you going to get the girl one, too?'

Stewart hid his smile. 'This is Amanda. She is staying with us, do you remember?'

'Oh, yes.' Her expression said she didn't but that it wasn't worth worrying about. 'Sophie said "Nana" today. Isn't that wonderful?'

Amanda smiled. 'Yes, it is. She is learning quickly.'

'My boys talked early.' Leanore nodded her head with pride. 'It's a family thing. What did you say your name was?'

Stewart watched Amanda. She was pale but remarkably composed considering the worry she had for her daughter and the upheaval in her life. She coped with his mother's lapses in memory easily and without the fuss some people felt they had to make.

What a gap there would be in the household when Amanda left. He crossed the room and poured his mother a sherry. The more he saw Amanda in this setting, the more he wanted her here for good. Why did she have to leave?

'Would you like a drink, Amanda?'

She smiled at him and his stomach contracted. 'Tonic and lime, thank you.' Maybe it was better that she left and he began to get used to the emptiness he knew he would feel.

Not surprisingly the conversation changed to

Sophie and only Sophie as Leanore repeated the highlights of the day concerning her new granddaughter.

Stewart caught Amanda's eye with a conspiratorial grin and she smiled back.

Stewart admired her for that. This slip of a woman had more strength and bravery than ten men of his acquaintance. When he remembered how determined she had been to survive the train wreck he shouldn't be surprised she wouldn't balk at living alone with a prem baby.

How many other women would suggest leaving a comfortable haven because she needed to take responsibility he could easily have shouldered?

He wished she would lean on him more. He wished a lot of things, and none of them had to do with Amanda leaving. He allowed the conversation between his mother and Amanda to flow over him. Tomorrow he would arrange as much as she would allow him to, and at least he would know she was safe.

Amanda stepped into the narrow hallway of her aunt's house and the patterned wallpaper brought back myriad memories of life with Aunt Millie.

Even the smell of the old red hallway runner made her smile, despite the stains that looked less than inviting. She'd have to put down new carpet or just polish the floorboards before Simone came home.

Yes, it all was a little tattered around the edges and Millie had been gone more than two years but she acknowledged sadly she didn't feel as welcomed by the house as she'd expected.

No doubt the run of previous tenants had contributed to that and she wished she'd arranged the letting herself and not left it to Craig's indifferent attention, as he'd suggested.

It was too late now and she needed to see what she could do to prepare for her arrival and that of Simone in a few weeks.

A black burn mark around the light switch made her wince and the age of the stove and fridge in the kitchen reminded her that Millie hadn't liked change.

Still, she would be fine. It wasn't grand like Stewart's house but she had a roof over her head and no doubt she would be able to vastly improve it before she moved in.

The doorbell rang and she glanced at her watch. She'd been here half an hour already and Stewart's handyman was due. She wished now she hadn't given permission for him to come—she really didn't want Stewart to know how rundown the house was.

'Come in, Hans.' She gestured past her into the hallway and the efficient little Dutchman bounced in with his tape measure and notebook.

'May I have a quick scout around and meet you here in a few minutes perhaps?' Hans's eyes darted from the frayed carpet to the mould stains on the ceiling.

'Sure.' She watched him go and thought about the

few pieces of furniture she had in storage. Most of it was Aunt Millie's, which she'd insisted she take to Brisbane and had furnished the granny flat under Craig's house with. She'd have to clean here thoroughly before she brought them back.

Even two years ago she'd wanted a small part of her life preserved and she wondered if she'd had any premonition she might need them in the future.

Hans returned and he suggested they step outside and sit on the back step overlooking the tiny handkerchief courtyard. Even the weeds between the flagstones looked sad but it was better outside.

'It's not too bad.' Hans smiled and spread his hands.

'Which house did you look at?' Amanda stared at him in amazement but with his words her spirit lifted.

'It's just stripping back. You need a bit of electrical work—I can do that with my brother-in-law who's an electrician—and I can do the touch of plumbing needed. If you pulled the carpets up and polished the floors, it would lift it no end. Strip the wallpaper and put on fresh paint, and if you like the floral look put back a floral border under the picture rail. Paint and borders are cheap and I own a sander. Know where a secondhand stove and fridge is, too, that's cheap and a lot better than the one in the kitchen. A thousand bucks and I could do it in a week.'

She couldn't believe it. She had that at least in her savings. 'Can I say yes quickly, and you won't change your mind?'

'No problem. I'll drop some paint charts and border books at Stewart's. I've a sneaking suspicion the floorboards are rosewood and will be beautiful.'

That evening when Stewart arrived home from work, he waylaid Amanda in the hallway. 'Hans says the house has potential.'

Amanda grinned. 'He's wonderful. Thank you so much for sending him round.'

'My pleasure to see you so excited.' He hesitated but decided to say it anyway. 'We'll miss you when you go. I just wish you would let me do more for you.'

Surely she was imagining the warmth in his eyes. This was not the first time he'd said something like that. He was a kind man who had some silly idea he was in her debt. That was all.

As if he read her doubts he said it again. 'I don't want anything to happen to you, Amanda.'

'That's just because you found me in wrecked train carriage and you think I'm a disaster waiting to happen.' She made light of his statement but it was warming that he cared. She'd never had someone there to lean on after her aunt. And even her aunt had leant on her towards the end.

But she was a big girl now. It was time to stand on her own feet again so she'd better not get too used to Stewart's strength.

'What if I hadn't met you? What if Desiree and I

hadn't shared the same carriage? I would be doing this on my own and there wouldn't be any Hans to help me set the house right. You've done enough.'

He pinned her with the intensity of his gaze. 'You did meet Desiree, you did protect my niece from danger and perhaps our paths were destined to cross. It's not unusual that I would like to help you and Simone.'

'It's too much to expect from you.' She needed to labour the point.

He smiled without humour. 'Oh, I know you don't expect it. Call it gratitude for your care for Sophie if you like but this is how it is going to be until I'm sure the house is safe. That's the end of it. On this I will not negotiate.'

Now he was being stubborn. Did it matter if she let him have his way? She was paying for the majority of the repairs and capitulation was no hardship in this instance. 'Fine. As you wish.'

'Thank you.' His voice lowered. 'There's something else we need to discuss. Desiree's funeral is tomorrow at ten. Apparently she had no other relatives and few friends since marrying my brother. It will just be my mother, Winny and myself. How do you feel about Sophie going?'

He continued to amaze her. 'Thank you for asking my opinion, Stewart. I think Sophie should be there, if only to have someone who is truly her own for Desiree. Sophie's too young to be upset and under-

stand and you will be able to tell her when she is older
that she was there.'

He nodded. 'I thought so as well. Will you come?'

She thought sadly of the young woman in the train.
'Certainly. Thank you.'

'That's settled, then.' He stepped back to allow her
to pass. 'We'll leave from here together at nine-thirty.'

CHAPTER NINE

DESIREE'S funeral passed simply but Amanda found it unexpectedly poignant. Amanda had needed Stewart's comforting arm more than she'd thought she would, even though she had the weight of Sophie's warm little body snuggled against her.

She felt like a goose when he handed her his handkerchief because she'd hoped he hadn't noticed her tears. 'I'm sorry. I barely knew her, I know.'

He hugged her shoulders briefly and took Sophie from her. 'Funerals are personal even if you didn't know the deceased well.'

Amanda wiped her eyes and blew her nose before she looked up at him. He looked tall and distinguished, and perfectly at ease with his niece in his arms, but she couldn't read any hint of his thoughts and she wondered what thoughts lay behind his blue eyes.

'It's the saddest event I have ever attended,' she said quietly.

His brows creased. 'Loss of life is always tragic.'

'At my aunt's funeral all her friends were there to say goodbye. We celebrated her life, had a slide show of her adventures, people told stories of the fun they'd shared with her. No one is here to celebrate Desiree's life.'

She sighed. 'Perhaps it struck me particularly because I've been a little too close to death myself. If Simone and I had died in the train, even fewer people would have been at my funeral than the five of us at Desiree's.'

Stewart nodded and she knew he understood. He gathered her in and they had a hug with Sophie between them. It felt wonderfully comforting for Amanda but she pulled away self-consciously. She looked across at Leanore and Winny but they were talking quietly with the minister and hadn't noticed.

Stewart smiled wryly and didn't comment on her distance. 'Death has been close to you. But you didn't die. Simone is growing beautifully, you both have a home at the moment and your own to look forward to. Next week you will start your job and move on with your life again.'

He was right. Even though home and job were temporary, she was back in control of her life.

Now that he knew how she felt, Stewart was encouraging her to be independent. Why was that a shock?

Amanda scattered a handful of rose petals on the fresh grave of a woman she barely knew and wished her peace. She took Sophie back into her arms and hugged her.

Two exquisite wreaths and a gorgeous spring posy were placed by the funeral attendant and the leafy tendrils drifted over the mound like a veil and covered the harshness of the turned earth.

'What beautiful flowers,' Amanda said, and wished she'd thought to at least bring a rose from Stewart's garden.

'The white orchids are from my family, the roses from you, as you were the only one of us who had met Desiree, and the posy is from Sophie. There had to be flowers.'

Amanda felt tears in her throat and swallowed them back. 'Thank you,' she whispered, but couldn't help the deep pang of guilt that she had survived and Desiree hadn't.

Amanda didn't want to go straight home and pretend they hadn't been to a funeral. 'Can we take Sophie to the park for a little while?'

Stewart glanced down at his suit and Amanda's delicate shoes but then he smiled and shrugged. As usual he understood. 'Of course. We've got two cars. I'll ask if Mother and Winny would like to come or meet us at home.'

Leanore said she was tired and they watched the older couple leave.

Stewart drove Amanda and Sophie to a nearby children's playground where Sophie was introduced to the delights of swinging in the safety of Amanda's arms.

As Stewart gently sent Amanda and Sophie to sail through the air he knew this was what he wanted.

Sophie's gurgles and glee made him smile on a day that needed smiles. Amanda had been right to suggest this.

He wanted days like this, years like this. The idea of more babies with this woman had become hugely attractive—he wanted Amanda by his side as his family and with his family.

He just didn't know if he could hold a woman like her and he didn't know if he could stand it if he lost her.

Over the next week, whenever Amanda visited the hospital or travelled away from Stewart's house she knew it was one step closer to the last time.

The night before she started her first shift in St Meredith's Neonatal Intensive Care Unit, Stewart called her into the library before the evening meal. 'Hans's brother would like to rewire the whole house. I think it is a good idea.'

It would stretch her budget and postpone her move. 'I can do it later when I'm settled.'

Stewart wasn't interested in playing it that way. 'I don't think so. Old houses burn down. I'd like him to do it. If finance is a problem, let me pay for it for the moment. I will keep a strict account but I would appreciate if you allowed me to do this small service for you. Then I will sleep at night.'

The idea of Stewart tossing and turning because her house needed rewiring was so ridiculous that Amanda had to smile despite how much she hated taking help from Stewart.

His chin was determined and she had to think of Simone. There would be babysitters there while she worked and she couldn't risk an accident. Just this one thing.

'You look far too composed to allow outside influences to stop you doing anything you want. But in this I will just have to say thank you. Besides, I'd hate to stop you sleeping.'

'That would be a change,' Stewart said under his breath, a comment lost in the arrival of Leanore and Sophie.

Stewart recognised the exact moment Amanda walked through the swing doors into the NICU and he accepted he had it bad.

He'd glanced towards the doors a few times before she'd arrived to start her first shift and there was no doubt his day brightened considerably when she entered.

She looked happy and confident in her new blue trousers and the teddy bear patterned shirt that the neonatal unit adopted.

Her thick brown hair was tied back in a clasp and

as she washed her hands at the sink he had to stop himself from drifting over to check if she still smelt like the lemon soap she favoured.

The nursing unit manager, not him, would welcome and orientate her to the ward, he mocked himself.

He liked the way she didn't immediately head for Simone's crib but waited calmly for the NUM to greet her.

'Welcome, Amanda.' Claire smiled at her and Stewart knew she would settle in fine. How ridiculous he should be nervous for her when she clearly wasn't.

Out of the corner of his eye he saw Claire show Amanda the staffroom, the sterile stockroom and the tiny tearoom, and they laughed together over some aspect of the unit he didn't catch.

He tried to remember if she had ever laughed so freely with him and vowed to work on his lightness. Sean would have known the right thing to say to bring a smile to her face.

He frowned. The last thing he needed was to go down that road again. Amanda had more depth than any of the women in his past.

He turned away abruptly, the moment tarnished inexplicably by his brother's shadow, and he almost ploughed into Gina.

She raised one eyebrow at him. Terrific. Now he'd have to strangle Gina or the whole unit would be teasing him for fancying the new girl. He scowled at her but she just winked back.

'My lips are sealed,' she whispered as she backed around a crib out of his way.

Her eyes met his and he actually believed her, but wondered at her motives.

Her discretion was a relief. His intentions had crept up on him and he didn't need to air them at work prematurely. Thinking of work, he decided he'd better do some.

For Amanda, her nerves about starting in the unit proved unnecessary. Everybody remembered her from her visits to Simone. She'd been welcomed before her first shift by most of the nurses. Her familiarity had also made it easy to find her way around, though now she knew the staff areas.

By the end of the first day Amanda felt as if she'd worked at St Meredith's Neonatal Intensive Care Unit for years.

Claire was even-tempered and fair and she wanted her staff to be happy. On the whole, they welcomed Amanda and nobody judged her if she spent a few extra seconds checking her daughter between tasks.

Stewart seemed to have the time to discuss most of the tiny patients with her so that she felt well versed on the individual progress of each baby and could feel herself a useful member of the team.

The only complication Amanda noticed came from a certain coolness from one of the night sisters at handover.

When she spoke to Gina about it, Gina laughed.

'Reba's had her eye on Stewart for a year now. She saw him make a beeline for you the other morning so she's letting you know how she feels. She'll get over it.'

Amanda's brow creased. 'He's Simone's doctor. Stewart is always very professional—caring but professional. I've seen him treat other mums with the same kindness.'

'Who knows what men think?' Gina said cryptically. 'But I can see you don't expect any favours from him.' She changed the subject.

'Have you seen the new linen man? He's cute in a mysterious way. Very intense eyes.'

Amanda laughed. 'You always have your eye on a new man. The last thing I need is a relationship. I'll tell you about my ex one day. They say you have to be burned before you fall in love, and this guy sure burned me.'

As she moved off she saw Stewart's brows rise and wondered if he'd heard her comment about romance. She shrugged it off and went about her business. She was soon too busy to worry about it and then there was the relief of Simone's progress.

Simone was gaining weight and tolerating her tube feeds brilliantly.

The patent ductus had closed after three days on the indomethacin and her anaemia had resolved with the blood transfusion.

Jaundice had only been a fleeting problem and

there had been no complications with her breathing since the early days.

All Simone needed to do was gain weight and establish breastfeeding when she was ready.

At three weeks old, or thirty-two weeks, she'd been moved down the unit to the less critical section. Her spot had been taken by twenty-nine-week twin girls that had arrived the previous day after their mother had had severe pregnancy-induced high blood pressure.

Delivered by Caesarean section, the girls would have died from the deterioration of their mother's placenta if they hadn't been born.

They would spend the next three months or so the NICU.

The babies' father, David, was standing between the cribs with a lost look on his face, and Amanda touched his shoulder. 'Kelly and Denise are both doing well, though it seems hard to see that when you see all the equipment around them.'

David turned to face her. 'My wife sent me down here so I can tell her they're fine, but they don't look fine to me. I've been here for twenty minutes and they still look like little aliens and now I feel guilty I don't love them yet.'

'You will. It takes time and you have had all the worry about Vicky on top of their birth.'

He looked unconvinced and Amanda went on. 'These little girls have a hard road in the next few weeks but if they have as few problems as it looks like they are going to have, you will notice the changes. They will grow rounder and more awake, and you will celebrate every change and weight gain like any parent.'

He nodded. 'But I feel so useless and they look so fragile.'

'Every new parent feels that when they see their premature baby for the first time. I did when my twenty-nine-weeker was born, and I've worked in units like this for years.'

David looked a little happier and she went on. 'When your daughters are stable we will show you and Vicky how to kangaroo-care your babies—that means laying them next to your skin. It is the most amazing feeling to see their breathing and heart rate settle to the best it's been because they are against Mummy or Daddy's chest.'

'What about all the tubes?'

'When their condition is stable, tubes won't stop it happening. Tell your wife that Denise seems to be the boss and Kelly has the most beautiful little nose. That's what I've seen today.'

He smiled and Amanda couldn't believe the transformation to his face. 'You are right!' He leaned closer and looked from one crib to the other. 'Kelly has her mother's nose and Denise has her determined chin. Wait until I tell her.'

Still smiling, he waved to Amanda and hurried off to see his wife.

'That was well done.' Stewart's voice drifted from her left and she turned to see him smiling at her over the top of a crib. He walked away, leaving her with a warm glow that stayed with her for the rest of the shift.

For Amanda it felt as if she had control of her life again. She was working, doing what she loved, and she was appreciated.

Claire had buddied her with Gina as both were very experienced and could handle the most complex equipment and situations. The two women generally managed the highest dependency end of the ward and few problems were insoluble between them.

Caring for the more critical babies also meant more exposure to Stewart. As each hour passed she came to appreciate his skill and compassion more as he dealt with his tiny patients and their terrified parents through the peaks and troughs of premature infant growth.

He met her at the door later that night after Gina dropped her home.

'You're late.'

Amanda smiled. 'Is this the start of a curfew?'

'I'm sorry.' He held up his hands. 'I meant, is everything all right in the unit? Come through and have some hot chocolate in the library.'

'Of course you did.' Amanda blushed as she followed him. She'd thought for a moment there he'd been worried about her and she needed to stop reading things into his naturally caring ways.

'It was the Daley twins,' she said as she sat down. 'Kelly was unsettled and David was there. He needed some extra reassurance. Since recognising resemblances to his wife he's relaxed a lot but now is terrified the babies will be sick.'

The room was gently lit and she relaxed back into the chair. This was lovely, she thought.

Stewart poured her hot chocolate and handed the steaming mug across before sitting down opposite her.

'I saw David pick up on your empathy. You being there will help him a lot.' He paused and sipped and then looked across at her. 'It has been hard for you with Simone there, hasn't it?'

'Everyone has been wonderful, but at the end of the day Simone is mine to worry over and wish that she were still safe inside me to grow.'

He nodded. 'It must be harder with the gaps in your memory taking parts of a pregnancy that was too short for you anyway. I wonder sometimes how hard it is for mums of prems to be suddenly thrust into a motherhood they weren't prepared for.'

'It's great if the paediatrician can see that.' She couldn't help but compare Stewart favourably to Craig again. There had been no way the mother's feelings had been a factor in Craig's care of his tiny patients.

She shook off the dark cloud thoughts of Craig left her with. 'I certainly never gave it enough consideration before I lived the situation. At least

Simone's birth will give me more skills when dealing with new mums.'

She sat back and sipped the chocolate. The liquid was rich and smooth and a wonderful way to end the evening.

So was talking to Stewart about things she'd only half formulated but wanted to think through. It was a shame they had done this because now she had another facet of their time together to miss.

'Are you happy with her progress?' Stewart broke into her thoughts and she forced a smile in his direction.

'Now that she is mostly out of danger, yes, though I do worry about her childhood milestones of walking, talking, and later schoolwork.'

Stewart sipped his own chocolate before answering. 'She's had lots of little problems but none of them serious. I believe she will do very well and you know I wouldn't say that if I didn't believe it.'

'I know. But it's the knowledge that Simone's brain had to finish growing in the bright, noisy, often painful nursery environment, instead of the peaceful time in my uterus.'

She shrugged. 'I know she'll need help with reading and comprehension skills and that I can help by reading to her from the time she comes home.'

She looked at him. 'My brain tells me that many extreme prem babies show very few problems but the worry is always there that I'll miss something.'

'You will do very well. She's a lucky little girl.'

They passed the next half-hour in desultory conversation and by the time Amanda went up to bed she was ready to sleep.

Stewart was nowhere near sleep. The more time he spent with Amanda, the harder it was to shift her out of his thoughts.

He loved the way she worried about others, and her determination to give the best care to her patients and their families.

He loved the way she cared for Simone and Sophie even though Sophie, wasn't her child. And he loved her kindness to his mother and even Winny.

In fact—he loved Amanda.

His feelings in the unit today when she had arrived, that warmth of pleasure just seeing her walk through the door tonight, and his relief she was safely home.

It was all more than he wanted to feel. It was the start of something he had never envisaged going though again, and he needed to proceed carefully because not only did she have no idea but he needed to learn to trust a woman again.

On Amanda's second shift she met Troy and Maxine, first-time parents of identical twin boys who had suddenly developed twin-to-twin transfusion at thirty-two weeks gestation.

Maxine and Troy had been invited to the unit to meet the staff before their babies were born and

Amanda had been allocated as one of their primary carers for their future care.

After the introductions and tour of the unit, Amanda decided the young couple looked more worried than when they had arrived. She sat down in the quiet room to answer their questions but was concerned about their ability to take anything in.

'How are you coping with the suddenness of it all?' She included them both in her sympathy.

They had looked so young and terrified in the unit when they had walked around she'd felt her heart go out to them. 'I know how frightening and distressing it is to have a pregnancy end before you expected it. This place seems pretty scary, I'll bet.'

Troy nodded. 'The babies are so tiny. Even your baby seems half the size of a normal baby.' It had helped a little when she'd shown them Simone.

'Your babies will probably be around her size, although one will probably be bigger than the other.' She pulled across a photo album of previous babies. 'I have a photo here of the last twins who had the same condition as yours. This is them at one year old.'

She showed the photo of two grinning babies, one slightly larger than the other but both obviously active and happy.

Maxine and Troy both smiled. 'Ours are boys, too!'

When she judged they were ready she showed the next page. 'This is when they were born.' She let the silence lengthen as Troy and Maxine stared at the babies. Both had intravenous fluids up and a tube for feeding in their noses. One was markedly larger than the other, while twin two appeared markedly pale and skinny next to his brother. 'The larger twin weighed two pounds four ounces and the smaller twin weighed one pound six ounces.'

Troy swallowed and chewed his nails before finally speaking. 'How long were they here before they could go home?'

'These babies left about eight weeks after birth. Home about the time they would have normally been born. The bigger one left a week before his brother but they are both well now. They were born a week or so earlier than your babies are now.'

Maxine cleared her throat. 'And can I breastfeed them when they get older?'

'That's very important and the best thing you can do. Your milk will come in a few days after your babies are born, and even the tiny amounts of colostrums there the first day will be given to them to help their intestines to work properly. I'll ask a lactation consultant to come and see you and explain it all before you go to Theatre so you know what will happen.'

Maxine shook her head as if hoping the whole scenario would go away. 'How could this happen? Was it something I've done during the pregnancy? I don't even begin to understand what is wrong with them.' Maxine's voice wobbled at the daunting spectacle of the NICU her soon-to-be-born sons would enter.

Amanda slipped her arm around the young woman and gave her shoulders a squeeze. 'It's OK. Just remember, if anything is worrying you, ask. Ask anyone here.'

'For the moment just know that twin-to-twin transfusion can happen with identical twins who share the same placenta and amniotic sac. You didn't choose to have identical twins so it's not your fault. Or Troy's.' She smiled to include the young father.

'In this case the blood vessels of their placenta allows blood from one twin to flow into the other. When blood flow is equal, coming and going, there is no problem, but if the balance shifts and one twin gains blood and the other loses it, complications can occur quickly. That's why they have to be born.'

Stewart knocked on the door and they all looked up at him. 'Can I join you?'

'Of course.' Amanda gestured to the spare chair in the room. She had a feeling Troy might absorb more if it came from a man.

Stewart shook Troy's hand before he sat down. 'Hello. I'm Stewart Kramer, the paediatrician. We met briefly earlier. I see Amanda's giving you some insight into how it is here.'

'It's pretty hairy,' Troy tried to joke.

'Absolutely. I think coming here first is a great idea. It's daunting when you've new babies to think of as well as this place for the first time.'

'So will the boys be OK when they're born?' Troy

turned to Stewart and Amanda watched Stewart's handling of the expectant father's apprehension. His voice held quiet confidence without sugar-coating the situation.

'In Maxine's case the ultrasound showed twin one with a sudden increase of fluid. The flow of blood one way towards twin one is definite so it is probable we'll deliver both boys by Caesarean section very soon before more complications can set in.'

Troy nodded and Maxine bit her lip. 'Our obstetrician said maybe tomorrow.'

Stewart nodded. 'Your next ultrasound will help him decide. The risk to twin two is lack of oxygen and nutrients as well as anaemia, unlike his brother who has too many red blood cells circulating.

Troy sat forward. 'Why don't they do the op straight away?'

'We have to weigh the danger to the boys now with the risks of being born too early.'

'Why does a day make that much difference?'

'Because of the steroid injections we gave to Maxine. They take a day or so to work and help prepare the babies' lungs for early breathing.'

Troy nodded and Maxine clasped her hands in her lap.

Maxine looked up at Amanda. 'Thank you. I guess it's pretty neat that we can think about all this before it happens, but at the moment I just want to hide.'

'Then that's enough for today.' Amanda smiled

and stood up. 'I think you will be wonderful parents and all this will make sense one day.'

Troy held out his hand. 'Thank you. Both of you.'

Stewart shook his hand again. 'We'll see you when your babies come down to us.'

They walked with the young couple to the door of the unit and when they had left Stewart turned to Amanda and smiled. 'I gather you introduced them to Simone?'

'It is handy having my own prem baby for show and tell.'

'She's doing well. As is her mother in her new job. Claire is very happy with you.'

Amanda felt warmth in her cheeks from his statement. 'I love it here.'

'I know. We enjoy having you. Now, I have to go. I'll see you this evening.' He touched her shoulder and disappeared through the doors. She turned back to her patients. It would be different if Stewart wasn't here—though in some ways it would be easier.

CHAPTER TEN

WITHIN a week of Amanda starting work in the unit, Simone had progressed to opening her eyes more frequently, and her face showed facets of her bourgeoning personality, which delighted Amanda and everyone else.

Amanda had agreed on three eight-hour shifts, Wednesday, Thursday and Sunday evenings. She had decided to work mostly in the evenings as it suited the Kramer household if she was there for Sophie in the mornings. Not that she'd be there much longer.

After two weeks of this routine, everyone was settled and each shift Amanda stayed back half an hour to enjoy the quiet time with her daughter.

Two nights before she was due to leave the Kramer household, Amanda was kangaroo-caring after her shift. She'd unbuttoned her blouse and tucked Simone's nappy-clad body in next to her skin with her fuzzy head nestled between her breasts.

Simone was making little sucking motions with

her lips, much to Amanda's delight. It wouldn't be too long before she might go to the breast. At thirty-four weeks she stayed awake for longer periods before she fell back to sleep.

Amanda looked up to share the special moment with someone and magically encountered the warm approval of Stewart's gaze. 'You're back late tonight,' she whispered, not willing to disturb Simone with a loud voice.

'How wonderful,' Stewart said. 'She'll be feeding soon.' His delight was genuine and Amanda felt the joy in the moment expand to include him. A strange ache, like his comforting arms around her shoulders, expanded into reluctant awareness.

The moment crystallised into a wonderful connection between them. He stood there, his strong features softened in awe at a sight he must have seen a hundred times but that touched him just the same. That was the kind of man he was.

He laughed when Simone turned her head and seemed to stare straight at him. 'Hello, cheeky,' he said to her.

With despair, Amanda realised she would probably always measure men by his standards and was a good way to falling for Stewart Kramer. She was a fool.

She needed to leave his house urgently before she did something stupid. She'd already blown one job by falling for the consultant, though what she'd felt for Craig was nothing like this knife-edge of insanity she was beginning to feel for Stewart.

She began thinking about what she'd miss when she moved. Not able to see Stewart at breakfast, or sharing Sophie's latest news, or smiling together over one of Leanore's often hilarious lapses. The idea of moving out and limiting contact with Stewart to work was disheartening, but she had to believe she was strong enough to do that.

He'd carried her long enough. Stewart's care had helped her survive those few fragile weeks when Simone's health had hung in the balance and Amanda's own body had been recovering from the shock of the accident and amnesia and her sudden catapult into motherhood.

Once Stewart and his family were missing in her life the huge gaps they would leave would be filled when Simone was well enough to come home.

No more late nights after work in the library where they had taken to discussing work and Simone and a myriad of far-reaching topics while sipping hot chocolate to help her sleep.

No more Leanore and Winny and the sometimes bizarre family atmosphere of the Kramer household. She was fond of both older ladies and they seemed to think she would be there for ever.

Leanore would gradually become more ill, and she wouldn't be there to help Winny or comfort Stewart. It was even sad that Stewart's mother would be unlikely to remember her having ever been there.

And what of little Sophie with her toddling walk

and tuft of hair that she wore sprouting out the top of her head like a little fountain with a bow? Amanda had grown to love the little girl and the wrench of parting would be a further cross to bear.

Sadness overwhelmed her and she couldn't help the tears that filled her eyes. An errant teardrop fell onto Simone's face, startling her from the doze she'd fallen into.

'What's wrong, Amanda?' Stewart's voice was gentle and she refused to look at him until she had control of that urge to throw her arms around him and never let him go.

One long finger slid beneath her chin and he raised her face to his. 'We need to talk.' His face was serious and he held her gaze. 'I'll wait until you are finished then we'll both go home.'

Home! Amanda's heart echoed the empty word and she glanced away from his searching eyes to the clock. She'd sat here for forty minutes already. She didn't like to keep Simone out of the crib too long and it was time for her to go back. Ten minutes later they walked together towards his car.

Once home, Stewart held the front door open for Amanda to precede him into the entrance hall. His voice was wry. 'Go straight through to the library. I think this is a night for a drink, not a sedative.'

Amanda stood in the centre of the beautifully furnished room and waited for him to come back from wherever he'd gone. Her hands were shaking and she walked to the mantelpiece and stared almost blindly at the photos of his family.

She couldn't believe she had fallen for Stewart. Relived the same mistake. Even though Craig had been nothing like the man Stewart was, she was still a nurse in the unit.

She would make arrangements to leave this house tomorrow. Her gaze lingered on a photo of a young Leanore, two dark-haired toddlers on her lap as Stewart's father looked on proudly.

How could she have been so stupid? She would never fit into these people's lives. She looked around the room at the long French windows and the tall mahogany shelves holding early editions of hundreds of books.

She would never have her photo on the mantelpiece with her illegitimate daughter beside Sophie.

'I can see you there.' He'd come up behind her and she spun to face him, unable to believe he'd guessed what was in her mind again.

She searched his face. 'What do you mean?'

He took her hand and tugged her gently. 'Let's leave that for the moment.' He steered her towards the couch and on the low table sat two huge brandy balloons. Shallow pools of golden liquid rolled in the bottom of the glasses and reflected the light.

'Come and sit over here next to me.' He drew her down onto the lounge beside him. 'We need to talk.'

It was all blurring through the mist in her eyes and she'd had enough of confusion. 'You said that before.' She didn't know what else to say.

He lifted a glass and pressed it into her hand. The touch of his fingers caused that whole chest-aching thing again and she shook her head against the sensation.

'It's just a nip,' he said, misunderstanding. 'I know you are feeding Simone, but have a sip to celebrate her progress.'

He lifted his own glass and touched it to hers and it made that perfect high note of fine crystal. They both smiled because the scene was so clichéd.

When she sipped the liquid the taste was like nothing she'd ever tasted before. 'Is this brandy?'

He smiled and looked down into his glass. 'Brandy? Yes. Fascinating yet formidable. Like you, Amanda.'

She sniffed. 'I'm not formidable. I'm very ordinary.'

'You are extraordinary.' He placed his glass back on the table and gently took hers from her fingers to set beside his. 'You are unlike any woman I have ever known. I think about you often, too much, especially when I should be thinking of other things.'

When he looked at her with admiration she couldn't fathom, she knew he wanted to kiss her, and she shook her head in confusion. Where had this come from? How could this have come about and she hadn't known?

She ached to feel his lips against hers but that he

suffered the same yearnings seemed beyond her understanding.

He took her hand in his and lifted it to his heart and the movement drew her against him. His jacket was cool against her cheek but the comfort of just touching him warmed her soul.

Slowly his head descended and with the first heat of his lips against hers, fleetingly she knew she was doomed to miss this man for ever.

No matter what came ahead, she would never regret this moment. But would he?

She pulled back. Hadn't she been here before, straight to first base when she should have hesitated?

Stewart drew her against him again until her head was against his heart and she could feel the essence of him, the reality of his being, his mortality, and with the sudden thought of that heart not beating one day—that even Stewart was mortal—it became un-important if this was a fleeting moment or the begin-ning of something that would go on for ever.

His chest was rock hard under her chin and his arms came around her until she felt immune from the world. If only this could last.

When next he kissed her she was ready and her mouth opened under his because that was what she needed. She felt the vibration of him saying her name and the sting of tears returned with the feel of his breath melding with hers. When he lifted his head he traced the damp lines on her cheek and she turned her head away.

His finger tilted her cheek so he could see her face. 'You're crying.'

She sniffed and pulled away but he tugged her back until she leant against his chest again. 'I'm still technically postnatal, for goodness' sake,' she said with an attempt at lightness. 'You're tampering with my hormones.'

He chuckled quietly and his chest vibrated beneath her cheek. She slowly smiled, amazed at the feeling of power that she could make such a man react this way.

'Now, why has it taken us so long to get here, do you suppose?' He smiled down at her and she couldn't believe the way he looked at her. She'd never had anybody make her feel the way this man could.

This was terrifying but delightfully addictive. She was a fool but would give away this moment to no one.

Amanda moistened her lips because suddenly she wanted to taste him again and she didn't know how to ask. She tried lowering her voice and on cue he bent his head to catch the words. 'We've been a little pre-occupied perhaps,' she said, and lifted her face to his.

'It's certainly been an action-packed month,' he whispered, and she realised he was staring at her mouth as if bemused.

His preoccupation with her mouth gave her the needed confidence to reach up and slide her arms around his neck. In response he lifted her into his arms and spun her around with a grin.

She'd always known he was physically powerful

but when he stood and lifted her as easily as if she were one of his babies she admitted to very non-feminist satisfaction.

'I just fancied spinning you in my arms.' He explained his action. 'And you feel as good here as I imagined you would.'

She was sure he could read the barely suppressed invitation in her face.

He swooped and gave one hard kiss before he lifted his face away. 'I think we need a chaperone to finish this conversation.'

Yep. He could feel the pull between them.

'Conversation? Is that what you call it?' she murmured, and pressed her ear to his chest in search of his heartbeat again. How had they managed to reach this point so quickly and so seamlessly? She had no will to resist and a great desire to be carried to his room, but she knew it wouldn't happen. There was sweetness in that knowledge, too, despite the hunger in her soul.

The phone rang and startled them both, but Stewart was the first to recover. He set her down gently and tucked in her shirt where he must have pulled it out. She didn't remember him doing so but could quite believe how it had happened.

Her cheeks heated and she hoped he didn't notice as he glanced at her. 'I'll always have a fetish for teddy bears after tonight,' he said softly, and moved to the window to flip open his mobile phone.

'Thank you for that,' she whispered to herself. She

loved him for making the interruption secondary to what had gone before.

Stewart's face was impassive when he turned back to face her. 'Maxine and Troy's twins are on their way. I have to go.'

It was for the best. Who knew where it could have led? She watched him leave the room and she lifted the glass to her lips. The brandy tasted like medicine this time and she put the glass down. She grimaced at the empty room as she listened to him unlock the front door.

She decided. This time tomorrow she would be in her own home. Alone. Tonight she wanted to just share a little more time with him.

'I'll come with you. Even if I just stand with Troy and explain things.'

'Are you sure? You must be tired after your shift.'

'I'd like to. If you get held up too long, I'll come home in a taxi.'

They drove through the night together and soon the soaring walls of the hospital came into view. By the time they arrived in the unit the twins had arrived and were being settled into their cribs.

Troy was there looking lost and frightened and Amanda was glad she had come, if only for Troy. She knew that was the most use she could be.

Night staff had the technical side of the admission under control and with Stewart there, they only had to follow his directions.

'What happened, Troy?' Amanda came up to him and his eyes fastened onto her familiar face with relief.

'Amanda, how great you're here.' He ran his fingers through his spiky hair and he looked more like a punk rocker than usual. 'It's all happened so fast.'

'Sometimes it happens that way, but at least you had a little warning.' She drew him to the side as more equipment was brought for the babies. 'I thought they'd booked Maxine's Caesarean for tomorrow?'

He rubbed his eyes and she saw that his hands were shaking. 'The night sister was checking the babies' heart rates and Toby's heart was beating too fast so they decided to deliver them now.'

'Toby? So you decided on names, then?'

He smiled at that. 'Toby and Thomas. Toby is the big one. I haven't had much of a look at them but I think they look a bit like me.'

'Lovely. Has Maxine come out of Theatre yet?'

'I'm not sure. They said they'd ring when she went back to the ward, and I said I'd come down here with the boys.'

'I haven't said congratulations yet. You're the father of two sons. You'll be busy when they go home.'

'I just have to keep reminding myself that they will grow and they will come home one day. I guess I'm relieved that the waiting is over.'

She caught a five-minute hand sign from Stewart and steered Troy towards the tearoom. 'Dr Kramer will come and speak to you in about five minutes, once they have the boys settled into the unit, and he's happy they are stable. How about I make us both a cup of tea?'

CHAPTER ELEVEN

THE next morning at breakfast nothing personal was said. Stewart watched Amanda across the table and apart from the occasional pinkness of her cheeks their time in the library might never have happened.

To be honest with himself, he'd never expected that she'd say she would stay, or that she loved him, or that anything had changed, except that he was more in love with her than ever.

Surely she could see that he didn't want her to go? Equally obvious was the fact she didn't want to be with him enough to give up her independence. Of course she wanted her own life.

Her priority would be to prepare for her baby's arrival home in a few weeks and devote her attention to her daughter.

There was no room for a needy man like him and he didn't like the picture anyway. She didn't need the burden of his family on her, his sick mother and Sophie, and maybe it was all for the best. If the truth be told, he had a lot on his plate, too. He'd do better to read his paper and leave her to her own life.

'Have you rung this morning about Maxine and Troy's twins?' Amanda's quiet voice broke in on his thoughts and he was glad to think about another topic.

'Yes. The boys are stable but twin two took a bit of stabilising. He's had a blood transfusion and improved quite markedly after that. Twin one may be the problem. His heart is enlarged but we'll see how he goes on medication.'

The conversation stalled and for once Amanda couldn't cope with the companionable silence that usually existed between them. 'I thought Troy coped very well with your explanations last night.'

Stewart smiled. 'He coped a lot better because he had you there. It was a good thing you came in with me. Often the parents get left too long before we can give them the support they need.'

'Thank you.' She hoped he didn't think she was fishing for compliments. She changed the subject, trying to get around to what she really wanted to say. 'I think Simone's turned the corner with her feeds.'

Stewart looked up again from his paper. 'She did well last night. There's no reason she won't continue to do well.' He raised that one eyebrow, the way he did so well. 'Was there something you wanted to discuss?'

Thank goodness. Now it would be done. 'I've arranged for the removal people to deliver my effects to the house today. I'm thinking of moving out this morning or this afternoon.'

She couldn't read any emotion in his face to tell if he was happy or sad she was leaving.

Even his voice was ambivalent. 'Is there a reason for this sudden rush?'

'I've been procrastinating for a week, Stewart.' He didn't look convinced and she rushed on. 'Maybe I need to go while I still want too?' Her joke fell flat because the truth of that statement was apparent to both of them.

'I don't have a problem with you staying.'

'Well, I do.'

'Obviously. In that case, can I help you with anything?' He seemed so impersonal she felt like crying, which was ridiculous.

'You have been more than helpful, thank you. Will you explain to your mother and Winny, please?' If she did, she would cry all over them and that would make Leanore even more confused.

They were talking like strangers, which was tragic when they'd been so at ease with each other previously. He looked at her and then nodded. 'Of course,' he said, and returned to his paper.

As soon as he'd looked away she stood up and left the room. She would go and see Sophie to say goodbye, and if she cried the little girl wouldn't ask why.

Amanda could feel his eyes on her back as she walked away.

* * *

Amanda moved back into her aunt's house after lunch and a chill wind flicked needles of fine rain that made the tears prick Amanda's eyes. Or was she crying for another reason?

Stewart hadn't wanted her to move out but for some masochistic reason he wanted to be here when she went.

'You could put this off until Simone comes home.' Stewart glanced at the sky as he carried her pitiful box of possessions and a picnic basket of food prepared by Winny 'to give her energy'. Judging by her reluctant consent she hadn't wanted him to come. He walked up the three steps to the tiny verandah and waited for her to open the door.

Once inside, he glanced around at the newly painted kitchen. 'Or at least have waited until the weekend and I could have given you a hand to shift things around.'

Why would she not want to be independent from his house, people she barely knew, who already expected her to be available to them for childminding?

What had he been thinking when he'd brought her to his home? In his defence it had been such a shock when he'd discovered the woman he'd been attracted to hadn't really been his brother's wife that he'd skipped the reality of her not being a part of their life at all.

So now she was going—gone, in fact—and he was here, holding her box.

'Put it down on the kitchen bench, Stewart.'

Amanda rubbed her brow. The last thing she needed was Stewart's imprint on her new home—the place where she would forget how stupid she had been to fall in love with him.

'I'm looking forward to settling in,' Amanda lied, still reeling from the knowledge she'd gone to bed with last night. She had fallen for Stewart Kramer even harder than she'd fallen for Craig, and she wasn't ready to trust any man.

She wasn't going to make the same mistake she'd made with Craig all over again.

He didn't look convinced she'd be happy and she pasted a smile on her face. 'Besides, the removal people will be here soon and the man's promised to do a little rearranging if I make up my mind in a reasonable time.'

'What woman ever did that?' His left eyebrow did its party trick again to accompany his words and she had to smile—a real one this time.

'Your misogyny is coming out again,' she said.

'I'm not misogynistic.'

'No, Stewart. Have a good day and thank you again for dropping me here.'

She knew he thought she was mad and the concept didn't confuse her.

When he drove away she shut the door and leaned back against it.

Well, here she was. The hallway stretched ahead of her, polished floors a beautiful rose glow and the pink border around the picture rail did make the entrance look wider then the three feet it was.

She wandered into the empty lounge room and realised that not only had she lost Stewart and his family but she'd lost the last of Aunt Millie, too. She was alone and the house echoed with her loneliness.

It had been the right thing to move out of Stewart's house because she needed to stand on her own feet. She needed to prepare for Simone to come home and they would have a wonderful time together.

Echo.

It just seemed empty because she had grown accustomed to the Kramer household with Stewart and Leanore and Winny and dear little Sophie. But they weren't her family. Simone was her family.

The beeping sound of a reversing truck pierced the gentle rumble of distant traffic and she hurried to open the door.

'Mornin', missus.' The burly removal man ducked his head to climb out of the truck and jumped surprisingly lightly down to stand beside her. He wiped his hand down his blue singlet and stubbies shorts before thrusting it out in her direction. Amanda shook his hand gingerly in case he crushed it.

'Let's go, then. Me little mate here, Fred, is much stronger than he looks. You just tell us where you want stuff.'

He was like a steamroller and in what seemed minutes the house was partly furnished and looking more like a home. When Fred and his boss had finished, the truck drove off and left her alone again.

Even with furniture, the house still echoed.

'I'm going to see Simone,' she said to the empty hallway, and decided she needed to get a pet. A clean one so Simone didn't catch anything.

When she entered the unit she sighed with relief. It was good to be back around people, and she tried not to look for Stewart. She needed her family. She needed Simone.

The unit was very busy with the extra workload from Maxine's twins and another new admission, and Amanda offered to stay and help after her visit to Simone.

Simone seemed lethargic today and Amanda supposed she'd tired herself with the feed from last night.

Amanda herself could have done with sharing another successful breastfeed with Simone to lift her spirits but that was how prem babies were. Two steps forward and one step back. She should have expected that. It didn't mean there was anything wrong.

She considered asking Stewart to look at Simone but he was busy with Maxine's twins.

Instead, she offered to do an extra shift. She may as well while she could. Once Simone was home it would take a lot more organising to get to work.

Stewart's eyebrows lifted when he saw her pull a teddy bear gown over her street clothes.

'Sick of the empty house already?'

That was a bit too close to the truth. 'Just helping out,' she said, and smiled blindly in his direction before heading as far away from him as possible in the confines of the unit.

At least she would be looking after the well babies today and that would keep her out of Stewart's orbit and the urge to cry.

By the end of her shift she was dreading returning to the empty house. It would all be fine once she was returning to Simone and a babysitter, but tonight she knew it would be a lonely place to go home to. She'd get used to it.

'Do you want a lift?' Stewart appeared out of nowhere and was the last person she needed to see.

'No, thanks. I've booked a taxi. He's coming in ten minutes.'

'Fine. See you, then. Take care, Amanda.' The look he sent her made the tears spring to her eyes again and she wished these postnatal hormones would leave her alone.

Two long hours later she was still sitting in her lounge chair at home, staring at the patterned border around the walls, missing Stewart.

This was how it was going to be and she may as well make the most of it. Before she'd met Stewart the idea of this haven, her own home, this new life of independence, had been the one bright light in her disaster with Craig.

She would make this work. She knew she could— she just didn't know if it was as important that she achieve that goal of independence any more.

The phone rang and its shrill insistence shattered the stillness in the room.

It was Stewart. 'I think you should come into the unit and be with Simone.'

His words washed a bucket of cold fear through her veins. When he said, 'She's running a fever and her respiration rate has climbed suddenly.' Amanda felt her breath squeeze in her chest.

'What's wrong with her?' Amanda's eyes darted around the room as she searched for her bag and keys while holding the phone in a death grip.

'She's picked something up. Some infection has taken hold and she's developed pneumonia. We've done blood cultures and swabs and started her on antibiotics. She's back on oxygen. I've sent a ward-sperson in a hospital car for you and they should be outside your house soon.'

Thank God, she thought. That would be quicker than a taxi. 'I'll be ready.'

When Amanda reached the NICU the worried faces of the night staff, especially Gina, who had been caring for Simone, raised her fear to new heights.

Her first sight of Simone froze her three paces away and she knew then that her precious daughter could die.

'Simone was deathly pale and her open eyes had that sunken, listless look that identified very sick children. The intravenous line in her arm was heavily bandaged and the extra monitors had all returned, as if she had just been born.

She looked limp and lifeless despite the rapid rise and fall of her chest inside the Perspex head box of oxygen. This was an ominous appearance she had never wanted to see on her tiny daughter.

'Amanda?' Stewart came up behind her and his strong arms pulled her gently back against his chest so that she was rigid against him, still facing the crib.

His voice was low and determined. 'The pneumonia was confirmed by chest X-ray. If it is bacterial, there is hope we should be able to beat it.'

'Should isn't good enough.' Amanda bit her lip until the pain made her stop. 'She was listless today. I saw that. I should have told you before I left.' Amanda craned her neck to look into his face before turning back to stare at Simone.

His voice rumbled comfort in her ear. 'The onset is very sudden. It's hard to differentiate in a prem. You know that. We wouldn't have done anything until she had symptoms. We've started treatment now.'

She craned her neck again. 'Look at her, Stewart, She could die.'

His hands eased down Amanda's shoulders to her

upper arms. They both faced Simone as he tried to infuse some of his strength into her. 'She's very ill, yes. But we're onto it. You and I will be here until she turns the corner and she is a fighter. Like her mother.'

Amanda dropped her voice so others couldn't hear. 'How did she pick it up? I'm so careful before I open her crib. So are the others.'

'I don't know. We'll never know. Somebody slipped up, somebody could have sneezed as they walked past when the crib door was open you know how it is. The balance is fine between safety and disaster with prems.'

'Of course.' She shook her head. 'I'm acting like a person who doesn't know these things.'

He turned her to face him. 'You're acting like a mother—and you haven't had the luxury to do that with all that you've been through. Stop being so damned hard on yourself.' He ground the last sentence out.

She looked into his face. She'd never heard Stewart curse before. She realised that he was labouring under the same destructive emotions she was. He felt responsible for Simone's illness as much as she did. The knowledge calmed her and she realised again how fortunate she and Simone were to have him in their lives.

But that was for tomorrow, or the next day, or as many days as it took for Simone to recover.

Tonight she would sit beside Simone's crib and

pray that her daughter would know her mother was there as the antibiotics helped her fight the vicious organism that had attacked her body.

Stewart was right. Simone was a fighter and she herself would have to draw on that faith to keep strong. Blame was futile.

For the next eight hours Amanda watched every change and examined every range in Simone's observations and vital signs. The chair was hard but that was good because it helped her stay awake.

Simone's respiration rate climbed, as did her temperature, and Amanda began to despair. Her oxygen saturation was falling.

'There must be something else we can do, Stewart,' she implored with her words and her hands and her eyes, and she knew Stewart wished with all his heart it was so.

'We've done all we can for the moment. If her oxygen saturation continues to fall, we'll have to start her on CPAP again. She'll need to be ventilated to keep going until the antibiotics kick in. Then it's up to her and the antibiotics.'

All he could do was lay his hand on Amanda's shoulder and pray with her that Simone would improve.

All through that long night the hiss of the oxygen and the staccato beeping of the cardiac monitor seemed to burn into Amanda's brain as she watched her baby struggle for breath. It was so hard for Simone, her tiny ribs flattening to help the inflation of her lungs, her sternum receding to force the air out. She was tiring and she began to gasp as Amanda clutched the armrest of her chest and willed her daughter to keep breathing.

'She needs help with her breathing, Amanda. We'll have to sedate her and tube her.' Stewart had come up behind her and she felt his warm hand on her shoulder.

'Do it,' she said, and stepped back out of the way as Stewart and Gina prepared the mechanical ventilator. The nasal prongs slid tightly into her daughter's nostrils and the inspiration hiss of the ventilator pulsed with the headache that pounded in Amanda's head.

They were back to square one and Amanda was so scared she felt faint with the fear. But she wouldn't faint because Simone needed her and she had to be right here beside her to ensure her baby didn't slip away.

Amanda couldn't stand not touching her. She slid her hand through the porthole and touched her daughter's pale face.

'I love you Simone. Mummy's here.' Her voice broke and she swallowed the fear and pain in her throat. She had to be strong for Simone. 'Keep going, darling.'

Imperceptibly Simone's respiration rate slowed a fraction with the help from the ventilator and at first Amanda thought she was imagining the marginal improvement in Simone's breathing. She continued to stroke Simone's face and dared to hope that her daughter had heard her voice and was responding.

There was no more improvement that night but at least she became no worse.

The sun came up and still Amanda stared through the Perspex of the crib at her daughter, willing her to fight the infection.

By three p.m. Simone had improved slightly but she was still gravely ill. Amanda slept for an hour in the little bed behind the sister's office and then resumed her vigil.

All the time Stewart was there in the background, except for the few times he had to leave for other appointments and an hour's rest here and there when he could snatch it. He was never away long and his registrar was there if he wasn't.

Stewart quietly circulated the unit, unobtrusive, aware of every nuance of Simone's condition, watching all the babies. Watching Simone. Watching Amanda.

All through the next night Amanda sat, willing Simone to survive. Simone clung to life like Amanda clung to the crib.

Finally, on the morning of the third day at four a.m., like the dawn threatening to tint the sky with promise of a new day, Simone began a gradual improvement.

Amanda saw it, Stewart saw it and Gina, who had been the carer overnight, couldn't help the hint of a smile on her face.

At five, as daylight drew nearer, Stewart appeared beside Amanda and brought her tea. Finally, there was hope.

It seemed Simone's improvement was here to stay. 'There won't be much more change before lunch. We'll look at weaning off the CPAP then. Come home with me for a few hours' rest.'

Amanda's head jerked off her chest from the doze she'd fallen into. 'I'm fine.'

'Hmmm,' Stewart said. 'Daylight is almost here and if you rested you could then come back refreshed later this morning.'

'I'm fine,' she said again, but she could barely keep her eyes open. Maybe he had something. She'd need her strength for the new day.

She heard Stewart's quiet sigh and it drew a fleeting smile to her lips. 'You're right. I'll go home.'

'I think you should come with me. I'll bring you back later this morning and I'm the first person Gina will ring if there are any concerns. You'll have transport as well.'

All perfectly valid reasons and her own reason for not going with Stewart didn't stand up to scrutiny.

She sighed. She hadn't been away from the Kramers very long but her reasons for leaving Stewart's house didn't seem valid when Simone's health was so precarious. 'Thank you,' she said. She was emotionally and physically exhausted.

She stood, stared at her pale daughter as she lay with a little more flexion than she'd had earlier, all small signs of improvement. She glanced over the range of readouts and, satisfied for the moment, she agreed.

'Be good, Simone. I'll see you in a couple of hours.' She blew a kiss in Simone's direction and allowed Stewart to lead her away.

CHAPTER TWELVE

'DRINK this.' Stewart poured Amanda a brandy in kitchen. His shirt was crushed and his hair was tousled from the long night. 'Excuse me for a minute while I make a brief phone call. I want an extra blood test from the last samples.'

He left to make the phone call to the unit and she stared after him. He looked so tired, as exhausted as she felt.

What would she have done without him? She guessed she would have survived but she and Simone were so lucky he'd found them.

The thought led to tortuous other avenues and she just couldn't unravel them now.

She picked up the thick cotton nightie Winny had left out on the table for her. She hugged the bulky nightie to her as if it were Simone.

Amanda glanced around the room she knew so well and sighed. She shouldn't have come because she'd never sleep, even though Simone was out of immediate danger.

Stewart returned and he glanced at her glass with a wry smile. 'You can lead a horse…' he said.

'Now I'm a horse.' She raised her eyebrows and he smiled at her irritation.

'Mule! Stubborn as,' he said. 'At least if you drank it, you'd have a chance of rest. You will be too exhausted to sleep.'

Her shoulders drooped and she held out her hand in apology. 'I'm not usually this pathetic but I'm feeling a tad vulnerable at the moment.'

He took her fingers in his. 'I'm not surprised.' The last comment was tongue in cheek and she shot a look to see if he was smiling. He was. She smiled back weakly.

His face returned to looking serious. 'I don't think another day without at least two consecutive hours' sleep will help anybody. I think going to bed, resting a little, and going back in a few hours could be the way to go.'

She nodded and then winced at the thought of lying rigid in her old bed, staring up at the dark ceiling, imagining Simone relapsing. If the phone rang, imagine if she didn't hear it, imagine if she was asleep and Stewart went back to the ward without her.

Stewart guessed her thoughts and his voice was sincere. 'I won't leave without you. Are you worried about lying wide awake in your bed, imagining the worst?'

He smiled gently. 'I am too! I'll be worrying about you as well as your daughter. Maybe you should come to bed with me. I could hug you dressed or I'll wear my thickest stripy flannelette pyjamas. At least I'd know what you were doing. I could even find a pair of flannos for you. We'll both think pure thoughts.'

She smiled at the picture conjured up by his words. 'Better than any chastity belt.' She smiled and couldn't believe that she had a smile in her, but he could do that. Make her feel things she'd never thought she would have the strength to feel.

The thought of lying in Stewart's arms, protected by his body and warmed by his heat when her heart was so cold with fear for Simone, was damnably attractive. Even in flannelette.

Maybe she would be able to at least close her eyes for a little while. He certainly wouldn't get away or make phone calls without her waking up.

'I'm game.' She looked at him. 'I really don't want to be alone.'

'You don't have to be,' he said.

They walked together up the stairs and she declined his repeated offer of pyjamas. 'Winny's nightdress will be strait-laced enough to subdue erotic thoughts.' It was wide, long and high-necked. 'I'm sure.'

Stewart mumbled something but she didn't catch it. Amanda was too tired to care.

Stewart watched her disappear into the bathroom to change and closed his eyes to block out the mental picture. He needed to keep his thoughts right away from there. He doubted a full set of armour would subdue his erotic thoughts but willpower would keep them under control.

After ten minutes, when she didn't reappear from the bathroom, he knew he'd find her indecisive behind the door. And it was so.

He knocked and entered the bathroom, and when she bade him enter she stood forlornly in the middle of the room and refused to meet his eyes.

'I'll be fine. Sleeping with you would be silly.'

'I'm deeply offended,' he teased. 'Please, don't tell the girls at work that you said that.'

Amanda looked up, surprised by the comment, and met the amusement in his eyes with a small smile. 'I won't, I promise.' She shrugged. 'I'm sorry, Stewart. I feel stupid to be so frightened Simone might relapse but I can't help it. It seems crazy for both of us not to sleep.'

He shrugged. 'I hate the thought of you lying alone and distressed. It would be a favour to me if I could keep an eye on you.'

He took her hand and squeezed it gently in his. 'Come on. Be brave and I'll be good. Maybe we'll both sleep. I truly believe there is more chance if we are together.'

Surprisingly, as soon as she felt Stewart's arms

around her, she snuggled in and went to sleep. But Stewart didn't.

His fingers curled into fists and he realised he would like to get a hold on whoever had not washed their hands properly or sneezed or coughed in Simone's direction and spread the damned germs.

He shifted uncomfortably. His brother, he could believe, would have thought nothing of settling a score with force.

Maybe there were demons inside both Kramer men? He'd always felt mildly superior to Sean, with his excesses and temper and penchant for trouble.

Maybe he, Stewart, wasn't so high and mighty after all, he mocked himself. Or was it he'd never had someone he cared as much about?

He thought about the time Sean had put paid to his marriage plans with Maria and enticed his fiancée away. Even then he'd been bitter and disgusted rather than violent towards his brother.

Amanda stirred in her sleep, and snuggled her warm little bottom closer into his groin, and he closed his eyes in despair. Not even flannelette was proof against that.

He tried to move away but she followed him with little seeking slides of her bottom and in desperation he pulled the pillow from beneath his head and jammed it between them.

Eventually he slept and dreamed vivid fantasies that kept the smile on his face.

When Amanda woke up, Stewart was spooned up against her and she judged it time to leave and save them both stress.

When she looked back at the bed, Stewart didn't have a pillow and she had two—one had been under her head and the other on the floor beside her. She must have taken it off him or else he'd thrown it past her in the night.

She crept out of his room like a guilty schoolgirl, a mass of nerves in case she ran into Winny, but nobody was in the hall and she made it safely to her old room.

The first thing she saw was the phone and she scurried across the room, snatched up the receiver and dialed the NICU.

'Simone has continued to improve. All the latest blood tests are improving and she only has a low-grade fever.' Gina couldn't hide her relief.

Amanda realised she was gaining a network of friends and that deep feeling of being alone seemed even more distant.

'Thank you, Gina.'

'No problems. We'll ring Stewart's house if there is any hint of a problem.'

'I know. Thank you again.' Amanda slowly put the phone down.

When she went down to have something to eat Stewart was already there.

'They said you'd rung,' he commented.

Amanda nodded with relief. 'She's continued to improve.'

'That's wonderful,' Stewart was smiling, too. 'I'll run you back in if you like but think about coming back here to sleep tonight at least until she is out of the woods?'

'Don't run me anywhere. I can catch a cab. I'm interfering with your routine.'

'It's my secretary who will be upset.' He grinned ruefully. 'I'll do the hospital round while I'm there and she can move a few appointments till later.'

The cereal felt like straw in her mouth. She needed to see Simone. Amanda put down her spoon. 'I can't finish this. I'll run up and get my bag. Do you think we could leave soon?'

'Of course,' he said.

She put her hand on his arm and looked up at him. 'Thank you, Stewart. You are very patient with me.'

He watched her hurry away and he knew that he would do anything for this woman. All she had to do was ask. But that was the problem.

When they entered the unit, Simone was awake and turned her head towards Amanda as her mother bent down to peer into the crib.

'Hello, darling,' Amanda said, and Simone's little lip quivered.

'She knows my voice.'

'Why wouldn't she?' Stewart slipped his arm

around Amanda's shoulders and hugged her. 'This evening you will be able to nurse her and with the CPAP gone and just the weaning off of her oxygen to go, she is really on the mend. If she continues to improve as much as she has overnight, you may even be able to try her at the breast again tomorrow.'

'I can't believe how much better she looks in just a few hours.'

'I said she was a survivor like her mum.'

That night at nine o'clock, Simone Edwards was weaned off oxygen again. Stewart was there, as was Amanda and a small group of neonatal nurse aunties.

Stewart placed Simone into Amanda's waiting hands with reverent care.

Simone turned her head and smiled at her mother. 'She smiled at me,' Amanda whispered.

'I think that's wind,' Stewart teased.

Amanda swallowed the lump in her throat and savoured the weight of Simone's frail little body against her breasts as tears streamed down her face.

'She's lost so much weight.'

'She's fine. She'll put it back on again. It's over now,' Stewart said.

'Thank you, thank you all,' she whispered, but it wasn't enough as she hugged Simone to her again.

Simone began to fuss, her little fist thrust into her mouth as she turned her face from side to side.

Amanda sniffed back her tears and gave her baby

another quick hug just to reassure herself she was safe. 'Look at her. She's starving.'

'Try her at the breast,' Gina urged, and Amanda looked up at Stewart.

He smiled gently. 'If she's well enough to smile after she scared the daylights out of us she's well enough to try a breastfeed. Even a few sucks will help her immunity.'

Amanda sat in the armchair and snuggled Simone up to her. When Amanda lifted her nipple to line up with Simone's nose, Simone's little mouth opened expectantly and as they watched she latched herself on perfectly and began to suck vigorously as if she'd done it a million times before.

'It's a breeze all the way from here,' Stewart said with a grin, and Gina lifted her fist in the air in triumph.

Amanda shivered as she looked down at her daughter. 'We were so lucky it turned out as it did.'

'Yes, we are.' Something in his voice made her look up at Stewart. It seemed as if he hesitated to say something.

'What?' Amanda raised her eyebrows.

'Later.' He shook his head.

'What is it?' She said again.

He smiled and his smile held a hint of self-mockery. 'I need a hug, too, but I'll have to wait.'

He was the type of man who would feel responsible, despite the fact that he'd been instrumental in Simone pulling through. Or maybe that flickering hope she'd hugged to herself was true. Maybe he did care? Or maybe he'd just needed comfort.

She teased him with a smile. 'I could call Gina back. She gives a great hug.'

'Not quite the provider I had in mind but I'll wait.' There was no doubt now what he wanted.

'I'll save a special hug for you. You deserve one.' Amanda glanced down at her now sleeping daughter. She held close to the warmth of the look Stewart had directed at her.

Just what that look meant for her and Stewart she would have to wait and see. The last seventy-two hours had been so traumatic she needed time to soak in that her daughter was safe.

She couldn't leave yet. She wasn't ready. 'Would you mind terribly if I stayed to the end of the shift?'

He shook his head and glanced at his watch. 'Of course not. I'll come back and pick you up when you finish.'

'I can catch a taxi.'

'I'll come back.' His tone was still quiet but she heard the edge of non-negotiation. In truth she didn't fancy the idea of walking out and waiting for a taxi after the day they'd had.

When they arrived home later that evening the light was on in the kitchen and Stewart came up behind her and steered her into the room. He kept his hand on her shoulder.

'Not a hot chocolate night?' She smiled past the butterflies that had started up as he turned her to face him.

'I think not.' He drew her towards the chair at the kitchen table. 'Come, sit with me and try to believe it is all over.'

It was true. She didn't have faith that it was over yet. 'How do you know?' She looked at the understanding in his eyes and shook her head. 'You're right. I can't believe she won't get sick again. So many terrible things could have happened.'

He squeezed her shoulder. 'But they didn't.' He sat down and pulled her onto his lap and put his arm around her so that she was nestled against him, warm and safe. 'It's been a long road for you and you have been amazingly strong for too long.'

Her throat choked with unshed tears. 'I don't think I would still be sane if it hadn't been for you. I'm sure it would have turned out differently if I hadn't had your support.'

Stewart shrugged. 'I believe life is like that and things happen in the scheme of things. You helped Sophie, I could help you…' His voice dropped and he caught her gaze. 'And in the end I'm hoping you will save me from myself.'

'I doubt you need saving from anyone.' She turned her head and lifted his hand to her lips to kiss. It was a crazy, impulsive thing to do but she just needed to do that.

He closed his eyes and groaned indistinctly.

Her eyes widened. 'Did I hurt you?'

He laughed faintly. 'I'm trying to stop myself from spinning you around and taking up where we left off last time. That little attention didn't help.'

She bit back a smile and resisted the urge to pick his hand up and kiss him again. 'I'll be good.'

'Damn.' He smiled. 'Let's talk about the immediate future just for a minute. Now that Simone is feeding, I don't expect many setbacks. Another week or two and she will be ready for discharge home.'

Amanda felt the floor drop away from her feet. She'd have to do something about that. 'Home?' She looked up at him. 'Lucky the house is ready, then.'

He shook his head. 'I don't know if you are deliberately misunderstanding me or I am very bad at getting my message across.' He sighed with exaggeration.

'What do you mean?'

'I had hoped you had found a home. With us.' He stared into her face as if hoping for some sign. 'With me.'

She couldn't just go on looking after Sophie and accepting his hospitality. 'I can't stay here. I have my own home.'

'It's really not big enough for me. I have quite a family that needs to come if I go.' The words were simple but the meaning shimmered into a hundred different shards of promise and her heart rate skipped. This couldn't be happening.

In the past, with Craig, she'd assumed before what a man had meant and she'd assumed wrong. She wasn't taking chances with something as important as this. 'Why do you want me to stay?'

He lowered his voice but every word was enunciated slowly and clearly so there could be no mistake that he meant what he said.

'Dearest Amanda. I love you. Have loved you from the first moment I looked into your determined eyes.' He rolled his eyes self-mockingly. 'I was most distressed when I believed you were my brother's wife and I was inappropriately attracted to you.'

'Inappropriately?' she said teasingly.

'Hmm.' He kissed her quickly to silence her. 'This is my speech. You have to wait your turn to ask questions.'

She settled back, unable to imagine what else he could say that could make this moment more amazingly wonderful than it was.

He held her hands in his and the seriously besotted way he was looking at her made her shake her head. This could not be happening.

He went on. 'I look forward to the first moment that I see you every morning.' He kissed her. 'Did you know that?'

She shook her head.

'When you are around my day is brighter and my nights hold a promise for the future I haven't given up on. I refuse to give up on. I can't imagine not having you to come home to. I hated the one day you moved out.

'So…' He lowered himself to one knee and she shook her head to implore him not to do that.

'I will do this properly for the first and last time in my life.' He stared up into her face and she could feel herself shaking. This was not happening.

His words settled around her like a loving cloak. 'Dearest Amanda,' he said again. 'Will you do me the honour of becoming my wife?'

He'd said it and there was no mistaking his sincerity. How could this have happened? She pulled his hands to make him sit beside her on the couch again. 'I come with a ready-made family of my own.'

He squeezed her fingers. 'So do I. I hope you don't mind.' She laughed. She supposed he did but Sophie and Leanore and Winny were all bonuses.

He went on. 'I love you. I would be proud to call Simone my daughter. I will be even prouder to call you my wife.'

For the first time he looked unsure of himself and she felt the tears in her throat, but for the life of her she couldn't speak. Answer him, her brain screamed.

The words tumbled out and all she wanted to do was kiss him for making all her dreams come true. 'I would be honoured. I love you. I knew when I'd been here a week that I never wanted to leave. I didn't dream that you could love me, too.'

'Don't talk about it. How do you think I felt when

the dreaded love-at-first-sight experience was with my supposed sister-in-law? A very sobering episode that was.'

She couldn't believe that not only had she finally found peace and security in her new life but that Stewart loved her. It all seemed an impossible dream come true.

'What will your mother say?'

'She will be delighted. My feelings are beside the fact that I know my family feel the same.'

'When?'

'As soon as humanly possible,' he said and swept her into his arms.

The wedding was held on a yacht on Sydney Harbour a month later.

The gangplank was festooned with flowers and the bride drew gasps from the small crowd of well-wishers, mostly from the hospital, when she stepped aboard.

Stunning in a sheath of just-cream silk that matched her fiancé's tie, Amanda's hair was caught up with the tiniest veil that dusted the back of her neck and left her sparkling smile free to delight the onlookers.

She saw her husband-to-be, tall and distinguished, his handsome face alight with love and devotion as he waited for her, and she returned his look with her own love blazing for all to see.

Leanore sat beside Winny, who held Simone in her

arms, and wondered out loud what Stewart's bride's name was again.

The nanny from Brisbane, tracked down and enticed by Stewart to join them, held a laughing Sophie's hand and pointed out the bride.

Amanda turned to Gina, gorgeous as bridesmaid at her side, and passed on her posy of tiny violets, so that she could take her husband's hand and begin their lives as one wonderful family.

Stewart's fingers closed around hers and she knew that today was the start of something beautiful and she'd found the one man she could love and respect for ever.

Medical Romance™

COMING NEXT MONTH
TO MEDICAL ROMANCE SUBSCRIBERS

Visit www.eHarlequin.com for more details

Desert Doctor, Secret Sheikh by Meredith Webber
Dr. Jenny Stapleton has devoted herself to those in need around
the globe, risking her life but never her heart. Then, in Zaheer,
she meets Dr. Kam Rahman. But Kam is not just a doctor—he's a
sheikh! Sheikh Kamid Rahman is soon to ascend the throne, and
he wants this desert doctor as his queen!

A Single Dad at Heathermere by Abigail Gordon
The pretty village of Heathermere is not only a home but also a
sanctuary for Jon Emmerson and his young daughter, Abby. Here
he can simply focus on being a father and the local doctor, leaving
his past far behind—until the day he bumps into childhood friend
Dr. Laura Cavendish. Laura is a struggling single parent, too, and
before long Jon realizes they are meant to be a family.

The Italian Count's Baby by Amy Andrews
Nurse Katya Petrov believes her unborn baby really needs its
father. But talented Italian surgeon Count Benedetto, with whom
she spent one passionate night, has no idea she is pregnant. Once
he finds out, though, it becomes clear that he wants to be a father
to his child, and he offers Katya marriage—for the baby's sake! But
Katya secretly longs for Ben to one day give her his heart, as she
has already given him hers.

The Heart Surgeon's Secret Son by Janice Lynn
Nurse Kimberly Brooks has postponed her week-long training
session with leading heart surgeon Daniel Travis once already.
Even though she feels like running for the hills, she can't put it off
any longer. She has to go into surgery and face the man she once
loved with all her heart. But, as the week goes on, Kimberly feels
the pressure of her renewed feelings for Daniel, and of her untold
secret—he is the father of her son.

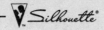

SPECIAL EDITION™

INTRODUCING A NEW 6-BOOK MINISERIES!

 THE WILDER FAMILY
Healing Hearts in Walnut River

Walnut River's most prominent family,
the Wilders, are reunited in their struggle to
stop their small hospital from being taken over
by a medical conglomerate. Not only do they
find their family bonds again, they also find love.

STARTING WITH

FALLING FOR THE M.D.

by *USA TODAY*
bestselling author

MARIE FERRARELLA

January 2008

*Look for a book from The Wilder Family
every month until June!*

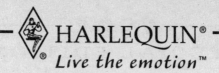

Silhouette®

Desire

NEW YORK TIMES BESTSELLING AUTHOR

DIANA PALMER

A brand-new Long, Tall Texans novel

IRON COWBOY

Available March 2008
wherever you buy books.

USA TODAY and international bestselling author Penny Jordan brings her famous passion and drama to these four classic novels.

Available in March wherever books are sold, including most bookstores, supermarkets, discount stores and drugstores.

www.eHarlequin.com

RCBOPJ0308